GIFT FROM THE APACHES

Turning toward the saloon, Calhoun halted, puzzlement coming into his face. Standing in the middle of the street, their heads toward Weymarn's Trading Post, were three dogs.

Their hackles were up and two were barking savagely while the third lifted his muzzle to the morning sky in a wild howl. Slowly, cursing softly, Calhoun limped toward the dogs. "What the hell's the matter with you boys?"

Calhoun hobbled toward the steps and was on the veranda facing the trading post door when he saw the object lying against the doorsill. For a stunned moment there was puzzlement in Calhoun's face, and then he understood.

The object was wrapped in dirty cloth; it was a severed white man's arm holding a silver dollar in its unclenched fist.

Dell Books by Luke Short

SUMMER OF THE SMOKE

THE SMOKE

Luke Short

A DELL BOOK

1

This was the summer the smoke talked. It was Apache talk from mesa and mountain and for the handful of people in tiny Weymarn's Crossing—too near the reservation, too far from the nearest military post. It was a time of unease and alertness.

For Maco, the young Apache renegade, had spent the early summer behind bars in Fort Kelso. The older Indians, hating trouble, were relieved at his arrest but the young bucks were full of wild and restless talk which the smoke lifting against still and brassy skies transmitted. Rumor had said everything and was even rounding on itself so that the Crossing, only yesterday, had heard from a passing freighter and didn't believe that Maco had broken loose from the post jail.

In the still heat of noon the blacksmith's forge and anvil behind Weymarn's log trading post was silent, but its clamor was exchanged for the dry rasping chorus of the locusts among the cottonwoods along the creek. However, a careful listener would have heard the rasping diminish and then die as a handful of Cavalry troopers on slogging, dusty horses wearily approached the ford and let their horses drink from the stream.

The lieutenant in command eyed the dozen log houses, the big trading post and its adjoining saloon with worried concern. Then, seeing a pair of sheets hanging on the clothesline behind the nearest house, his lean face relaxed a little.

"Don't let them drink too much right now," he called over his shoulder to his men. Lieutenant Benson roweled his reluctant horse out of the water and the troopers fell in line after him.

One horse with its rider, however, remained drinking in the hock deep water. The rider would have been a tall man if he were not slumped in his saddle so that his head almost touched the horn which his hands clenched. His calico shirt was sun-faded where it was not stained with sweat. Around his right thigh, over the butternut trousers, the sleeves of a buckskin jacket were tied, the jacket itself trailing below the stirrup dripping blood, drop by slow drop, into the water.

Rising in his saddle Lieutenant Benson called angrily over his shoulder, "Carney, go back and lead Calhoun's horse out of there!" He halted and the indifferent troopers sat motionless, not even looking back.

Trooper Carney put his horse back into the stream and reined up alongside Calhoun. When he gently pulled the reins from his hands, Calhoun roused and looked at him. His eyes, black under thick brows, were brilliant with fever, and his gaunt face was flushed and salt-rimed from dried perspiration.

"What is it, old-timer?" he whispered.

"I'll lead your horse. It's only a little ways now."

"To where?"

The trooper shook his head. "It's just up yonder."

Calhoun's head sank. "It better be," he whispered.

The column was in motion again and the sound of this many shod horses in the noon quiet brought a girl to the door of the cabin where the sheets hung on the line. It passed other cabins where people watched from the door and then it was abreast Weymarn's Trading Post. Behind it the people whose houses it had passed came rapidly into the street and straggled up to the troopers whom Benson had ordered to dismount. By the time the bone-weary men had swung out of the saddle a dozen men—all of them armed, Benson noticed—were collected on the low veranda of the post. Others came straggling from downstreet.

"Looks like you got jumped, Lieutenant," one of the men said.

"That we did," the lieutenant replied curtly. He looked around the circle of people and then said, "I've got to drop off a couple of hurt men. Can anybody here put them up and take care of them?"

Almost as if by signal a good half of the townspeople turned their heads to look at a man who was leaning against the log wall of the post. He lounged easily with the heel of one boot hooked over the second log, the other thick leg propping him up. He was a wide man, both across and through, of average height, perhaps fifty, dressed in oft-washed and well-worn range clothes. His wide, weathered brown face was bisected by white mustaches stained brown at the corners of his mouth. Below the rim of his sweat-stained Stetson thick pepper-and-salt hair burred out; his heavy eyebrows were blacker than his dark eyes and were joined above the bridge of his short nose. This was Will Weymarn, after whom the Crossing was named.

He pushed away from the wall and lazily moved to the edge of the veranda. Looking over the crowd, he said one word, "Anybody?"

"I will, but for pay," a man's voice replied.

Lieutenant Benson looked at the speaker. He was a high-shouldered, pale-faced man past middle age with a veiled truculence in his face and manner.

"I'd rather have a woman," Benson said.

"My daughter will nurse and feed them, not me."

"Hallie Thompson's a good girl," Weymarn put in.

"All right, you'll get your pay. It may take some time, but you'll get it. What can you do for them?"

"There's room in the wash house. She works there most of the day. She'll watch out for them and feed them."

Benson nodded. "Cooper, you and O'Brien go with this man. Lead Calhoun's horse and don't dismount him until you have to." His glance shifted to one of the troopers. "Ryan, how's your arm?"

A tall, red-haired trooper, his arm in a neckerchief sling inside his blouse, shrugged indifferently.

"You go with him, too," Benson said. "I'll be over in a minute."

One of the troopers took the reins of Calhoun's pony; the man was sunk in pain, indifferent both as to what was said and what was happening. The wounded trooper and the second trooper followed.

"What did you run into?" Weymarn asked.

"Ambush."

"On the reservation?"

"Off, way off."

Weymarn observed quietly, "That means trouble."

Lieutenant Benson looked suddenly and searchingly at him. "What do you think we got now? Maco's loose."

The townspeople looked at one another soberly. Then the rumor was true. "You after him?" Weymarn asked.

Benson said bitterly, "I was until my guide got us in trouble."

"That the hurt man?" Weymarn asked, and Benson only nodded. Now he looked over the crowd.

"Is there anyone around here that knows the Big Salt Canyons?"

Weymarn's glance lifted and he turned his head to regard the crowd. His glance settled on one of the men on the porch, a dirty, pint-sized man whose roan beard came below the top button of his undershirt. In the place of his shirt was a pair of wide galluses.

"Barney knows them good, don't you, Barney?"

"I know them, but right now I wouldn't want to be in them if Maco's loose."

"How close will you take us?" Benson asked.

"So you can see them through glasses."

"All right, get your horse and war bag." To Weymarn he said, "Sell beer here?"

"Just whisky."

Lieutenant Benson turned to his dismounted troopers.

"Corporal, take over. Find some shade. Report any man who goes near that saloon or sends anyone for a bottle. Take my horse." Then he said, "Do that man and his daughter live at the end house?"

Weymarn nodded and stepped off the veranda, falling in beside the lieutenant.

"You figure the Indians know Maco is loose?"

"Sure they do," Benson said bitterly. "That smoke is as fast as any telegraph."

"When did you get jumped?" Weymarn asked.

"Yesterday."

"That puts them pretty close to us," Weymarn observed.

"There weren't enough in this band to bother you. Still they could join up with others. You'd better be ready for anything," Benson said wearily.

They turned into the gate of the pole fence that flanked the log cabin, skirted the building and then saw Calhoun's and Ryan's horses whose reins were held by the two troopers lounging against the wall waiting for orders.

"Tell your men to turn them into the corral behind the post."

Benson gave his orders and then stepped into the wash house. The smell of soapy water lay pleasantly in the air. Skirting the wash and rinse tubs and the stove, Benson hauled up and saw Calhoun stretched on some blankets in the corner. Standing beside him was a girl under medium height whose dark hair, pinned atop her head, was damp and curly. The sleeves of her plain dress were rolled up and her hands and forearms were still pink from the water of the rinsing tub. Benson smiled and nodded and the girl's answering smile was so shy that it gave her face a sudden fleeting beauty. Cap Thompson, standing beside her, belatedly said, "My daughter."

Benson touched his hat, said, "Pleasure ma'am," then looked at Calhoun and at Ryan who was sitting in a corner on his blankets.

Hallie Thompson observed then, "That's an awful hole in his leg."

"You dressed it?"

"Yes. Your soldier wouldn't let me touch him."

"Then you don't have to," Benson said.

Now he looked at Calhoun and saw a still unfriendliness in the man's fever-bright eyes and drawn face. It was a long weather-burnished face faintly shadowed with beard stubble and it ended in a squarish jaw that Benson now had every reason to describe as stubborn. Above a wide, narrow-lipped mouth was a straight chestnut-colored mustache; the eyes, as black as any Indian's under short-cut brown hair were recessed deeply behind jutting cheekbones. The nose, Benson guessed, had once been broken, since it was faintly crooked and he wished he'd been the one to break it.

He said, "I wish I could say I'm sorry I have to leave you, Calhoun, but. . . ."

"But you aren't sorry," Calhoun interrupted quietly. His voice was soft, slurred and sick.

"Not any," Benson said. He added, "I've had to hire another guide."

"Maybe he'll suit you better."

"I'm sure he will," Benson said grimly. "I wish you luck." His tone was formal and final and indicated the conversation had come to an end.

Calhoun acknowledged this by closing his eyes. Benson glanced at the redheaded trooper. "Ryan, if you want to keep that arm, you'll let this girl dress it. Also, if you'll just spend a half day in that saloon instead of a full one, you'll be all right. I figure I'll be back in three weeks to pick you up. You'd better be here."

He looked back at Calhoun and when he saw that the man was sleeping, he felt an unreasoning irritation. He, too, had been dismissed.

There was a lamp burning on the cold stove when Keefe Calhoun roused from sleep and he wondered what time of night it was. His fever seemed to be gone and he thought how enormously hungry he was as he listened to the deep, uncertain breathing of Trooper Ryan in the corner.

Looking about him at the mean room with the bark still peeling off its logs, he thought dismally, *I wonder where I am?* He could remember only patches of the day's events; a dark-haired girl had bandaged his leg, there had been two men in the room besides Benson and now he remembered his parting exchange with the lieutenant. He had been dismissed as guide and was not even paid off for his four days of service. While Benson was empowered to dismiss him, the lieutenant could not pay him. And that, Calhoun thought, leaves me with two silver dollars and a hole in my leg.

Now he remembered, this time without anger, of the cause of his dismissal. Lieutenant Benson's orders had been to pursue Maco, probably to the Big Salt Canyons, and recapture him. On the second day out of Fort Kelso, Calhoun had picked up fresh tracks and Benson had ordered him to follow them for an hour and to determine, if possible, whether the Apaches were near. It took Calhoun half an hour to find and watch an Apache camp long enough to determine that it held nothing but old men, women and children.

Back with the troopers, he had reported this to Lieutenant Benson, who immediately ordered Calhoun to lead the detail to the camp. When Calhoun pointed out that this side trip was senseless, Benson had become angry and insisted that Calhoun obey his orders. Calhoun had guided them reluctantly and as he rode he became increasingly fearful that Benson meant to attack the camp.

When they were close to it, but not in sight of it, and Benson ordered his detail to dismount, form a skirmish line and attack the camp, Calhoun's worst fears were realized. He simply pulled his gun and shot into the air as a warning to the Apaches. Benson had been furious and ordered his detail to attack on the run. When they reached the camp it was abandoned; the Apaches had simply dissolved into the landscape.

Raging with anger, Benson had burned the few sorry belongings of the band. He gave Calhoun a wicked tongue lashing which Calhoun accepted silently, content to know that he had spared the futile killing of these defenseless Apaches.

That evening the consequences of Benson's senseless destruction overtook them. The detail was ambushed as they were making camp. One man was killed and Ryan and Calhoun were wounded. Calhoun knew precisely what had happened. The able-bodied Apaches had returned to find their camp destroyed and their families scattered. They had acted promptly in the only fashion an Apache understood, and they were right.

A dog started to bark out in the night and a man's voice, rough and exasperated, cursed him.

Calhoun put his ear to the rammed earth floor and heard the tremor of approaching footsteps. Then someone stepped into the room. His vision was momentarily blocked by the stove and then a man he had seen before stepped around it, looking at him.

He was, Calhoun guessed, in his middle fifties, a lean, high-shouldered, angular man in shirt sleeves. His seamed face was pale, his wide mouth down-pointed at the corners, giving him an expression of almost belligerent petulance. His blue eyes, under tufted eyebrows, held only a shallow curiosity as he said, "Want some water?"

Without waiting for an answer he disappeared and returned in a moment with a bucket of water, a tin dipper floating on the water surface, and set it down by Calhoun's head.

Since he made no offer to help, only stood back and watched, Calhoun reached across his chest and filled the dipper, then drank, spilling most of its contents down his shirt front because he could not raise his head.

"You're not the one that fixed me up," he said then.

"My daughter."

"My name's Calhoun."

"I already know that. Got enough blankets?"

"Yes. Where is it I am?"

"Weymarn's Crossing."

"No, this place?"

"You're in Cap Thompson's wash house. Good enough for you?"

His immediate sourness brought a faint stirring of anger in Calhoun, but he did not figure he was in any position to show it. Was this shack and this unfriendly man the best Lieutenant Benson could do? It was probably the best he wanted to do, Calhoun reflected.

He did not hear the daughter approach and neither, it seemed, did her father. She suddenly appeared beside her father, a tray of steaming food in her hands.

"What have you got there, Hallie?" Cap demanded.

"Soup," Hallie said almost timidly.

"Since when do we serve meals at midnight?" Cap asked sourly. "The trooper's snoring, and"—he gestured toward Calhoun—"his eyes are already half shut."

"Dad, it was still warm and I thought they'd like it."

Cap didn't even look at Hallie, only regarded Calhoun with dislike. "All right, but let's get this straight. We contracted to feed and nurse you two. My daughter isn't standing over a stove all day cooking food to stoke into you."

"I don't recall asking her to," Calhoun said wearily.

Hallie said pleadingly, "Let him drink his soup and go to sleep. This can wait until tomorrow, Dad."

But Cap went on implacably, "Oh, no it can't. I want to settle this now. Did I hear that lieutenant fire you? Is that what he meant?"

"That's right."

"Then who pays for you?"

"What did the lieutenant say?"

"He only said 'We'll pay. You'll have to wait, but we'll

pay.' But if he fired you, does that mean they'll still pay for you?"

Wearily Calhoun said, "I don't know."

"I don't know either," Cap said sourly. "I do know one thing though. We can't nurse and board a man for nothing."

"All right," Calhoun said.

Hallie, tired of holding the tray, crossed between her father and Calhoun and set the tray on the floor. As she rolled up the extra blanket and gently raised Calhoun's head he got his first clear look at her. The tiredness that was in her face could not obscure or alter the serenity of her gray eyes; her mouth was full-lipped and wide under a small nose that held a scattering of tiny freckles over its high bridge. Her black hair was swept back in two clean wings to the ribbon at the nape of her neck. She could have been twenty, no older, and Calhoun would have described her as slight, although her figure under her drab dress was full-breasted and mature.

When Hallie set the bowl of thick potato soup and fresh bread beside him, Calhoun forgot his pride; he wolfed it down and only afterwards realized that Cap Thompson had left the room.

When he had finished, Hallie, who was kneeling and fussing with the blankets at his feet, gestured toward Ryan. "He's sleeping, so why don't you eat his too?"

Calhoun didn't pretend he shouldn't or couldn't; he ravenously cleaned up Trooper Ryan's portion, also. Finished, he lay back, wiped his mouth with the back of his hand and looked at Hallie. He surprised a look of watchful tenderness in her face that was replaced by a shy smile.

"It wasn't much of a supper. I'll do better."

"You couldn't."

She shook her head, as if gently denying this. Then her face sobered and she stood up and her features, with the lamp behind her, were again dim.

"I'm sorry about Dad. He isn't mad at you. He just doesn't know if the Army will make good for you."

"I wish I could tell him. I guess I wasn't in any shape to talk room and board with the lieutenant." He paused. "What does your father do?"

He caught the hesitation before she answered. "No regular work. He has an old wound that troubles him too much for heavy work. He mends harness and—and does small light work." She added softly, "We're very poor. That's why this business of yours concerns him."

"It should."

She hesitated again. "Maybe you could tell us something. Does the Army expect the Apaches to break out?"

"They wish they had the answer to that themselves." Calhoun's voice was dry. "If Maco makes good his escape he'll take the young bloods with him. That will mean real trouble from here clear into Mexico. Maco's a born leader, cruel as a wolf, and the young men will follow him."

"Do you think the Army will get him?"

"No," Calhoun said quietly.

"Why don't you?"

"Because I just served under the officer for one of the two detachments looking for him. He didn't care about catching Maco. He was only interested in shooting Apaches—any Apaches. Do that often enough to anybody and they'll fight. They don't have to be Apaches."

The girl was quiet a long time. "Oh, I'm sick of it!" she said suddenly, her voice soft and bitter. "I work all day with a rifle at my elbow. We're the first house and if they come from the west, we're first. Every time Dad leaves the house I start to shake! I don't know whether I'm shaking for fear he won't come back or for fear they'll come when I'm alone!"

Calhoun was silent a long moment and it was so still he could hear Ryan's breathing. He suddenly felt sorry for the girl and wished he could comfort her. Then he said, "Look at it this way. The Apaches only go for a sure thing. If there are forty rifles in this town they'll think a long time before attacking it."

"But if they have a hundred?"

"Yes, there's that," Calhoun said quietly.

He heard her sigh and he felt a swift pity for her. This was no country for a woman. Were they too poor to move to a bigger town where sheer numbers would ensure safety, he wondered?

"I won't keep you up. Your holster and shell belt are in the corner."

She bid him good night and took the lamp with her as she went out. Calhoun lay there staring into the darkness, wondering at the curious mixture of shyness, fear and gentleness in this girl whose father seemed nothing but a blustering bully.

He hadn't been quite truthful with her when he said he didn't know if the Army would pay for him. He was sure they wouldn't, but if he'd said so he would have embarrassed her and angered her father. If he'd been wounded reasonably close to a military post, the Army would have taken him in and nursed and fed him. But this was different; he'd been hired to guide a group of soldiers from one place to another, and if he got hurt and couldn't, why should the Army pay for him?

Remembering the two silver dollars, he then remembered that he had a horse, saddle and rifle which could be sold. He rejected the idea immediately and instead thought *I've got to get out of here.*

Next morning Calhoun and Ryan were wakened by a stranger bringing them their breakfast. He was a man of thirty-five, stocky, with a long sober face capped by great tufts of pale eyebrows and he was dressed in worn range clothes and an old and formless hat.

"If you can't come and get it, I'll bring it to you," he announced. "I'm Sam Avery."

Calhoun said hello, and Ryan only grunted. Gingerly, Calhoun shoved himself up into a sitting position and gently flexed his leg. It was sore, but the stinging salve and tight bandage Hallie had used had turned real pain into a gentle ache.

As he ate, he watched Avery busy himself shoving kindling into the stove and building a fire. "You work for the Thompsons?" Calhoun asked curiously.

"No, I just help Hallie out sometimes. She's got a big load of wash today. But that's her living and she's not complaining."

"Her living?"

"She takes in wash. This is kind of a bachelor town, and then she gets trade from the ranches that haven't got womenfolks."

So that's it, Calhoun thought. *She's carrying Cap on her back too.*

Ryan spoke then for the first time and sullenly. "We get any coffee?"

"Right away," Avery said. "I'll get the pot and put it on the stove soon's I get the fire started."

He went out and now Calhoun studied Ryan. His face was flushed, as if with fever, and Calhoun heard his soft grunting whenever he moved.

"How's the arm?"

"Sore."

"You must not like it much."

"What? My arm?" Ryan looked puzzled.

"Yes, or you'd let that girl dress it before they have to tie you down and saw it off."

Ryan glared at him and then said, surprisingly, "Maybe you're right. I'll go up to the house after I eat."

As he ate, Calhoun looked around the room, knowing what he needed but not knowing how to get it. His glance roved to the far corner and settled upon a clutter of garden tools which he regarded for a moment before returning to his breakfast.

Avery came with the coffee and left, and when Ryan was finished his second cup he hoisted himself to his feet. "I'll go see that girl now," he announced.

He was starting for the door as Calhoun said, "Take a look at those tools in the corner, Ryan. Is there a hoe there?"

Ryan halted, looked at him quizzically, then moved past the wash bench and picked a hoe from among the tools. He came back now, a frown on his broad face. "What you want this for?"

Calhoun didn't answer. He held out a hand and said, "Give me a hand up, will you?"

Ryan leaned the hoe against the wall then extended his good hand which Calhoun took.

"Easy now," Calhoun said.

Slowly Calhoun raised himself, and the pain, quiet before, came immediately. It was an exquisite soreness rather than real pain and once he was standing on his good leg he knew he could bear this easily. His free hand bunched his jacket and now, leaning against the wall, he put the jacket in his armpit, reached for the hoe, tucked the blade under the jacket and leaned on his improvised crutch. This'll get me out of here anyway, he thought narrowly. He tried a step. Holding his hurt leg off the floor he could hobble reasonably well and under Ryan's gaze he slowly circled their sleeping space. The heat of the room was almost stifling and now he held out a hand.

"If you'll hand me my hat, I'll be all right."

Ryan picked up his dusty, battered Stetson in the corner, handed it to him and then said, "If you're all right, I'm going up to the house."

Calhoun nodded, waited until Ryan was outside and then slowly hobbled to the door and into the back yard. The back door of the house faced in the direction of the post and Calhoun could see Ryan standing at it, talking. Then Ryan, apparently by invitation, stepped into the house. Slowly then Calhoun made his way around the other side of the house up to the front gate, turning toward the trading post. His leg was throbbing regularly so that the bright sun of the sweet morning was a matter of indifference to him.

Laboriously, halting often, he hobbled down the street that was just receiving the spare morning traffic of wagons and an occasional rider. During one of his halts he carefully studied the town. It really wasn't a town, but only a settlement, he decided. The big two-story log trading post he was approaching was the biggest building here, and across the street from it four small log cabins. The post and saloon were on a corner and beyond the crossroads were more cabins, some of them new. They would be the buildings thrown up by the isolated ranchers wanting the protection of a settlement for their families against the Apaches, he supposed. There were perhaps a dozen cabins in sight and some of them nestled snugly under the random giant cottonwoods that dotted the settlement. To his left, he could see the low foothills beginning; they were dry and rocky, stippled with cedar and piñon, that would give way farther west to the timbered mountains. All of it was Apache land once. And might be again, he thought.

Moving again, he aimed for the post. His crutch was awkward but serviceable, yet the blade, even through the buckskin, dug into his flesh. He knew a hoe handle minus its blade could serve him better if the post stocked them.

Approaching the post, he saw a heavy man of fifty or so slacked comfortably in one of the barrel chairs on the railless veranda. Calhoun had a feeling that he had seen this imposing man yesterday sometime, but he couldn't be sure. He was a big, wide man with grizzled hair, black brows, a white full mustache and a cleft in his chin so deep it might have been made with an ax. The man watched him as Calhoun approached the three veranda steps, then rose and came toward him.

"Help you, Calhoun?" the man asked pleasantly.

Calhoun reached out for the veranda post, steadied himself and said, "Reckon I'll make it all right." Slowly, painfully, he climbed the steps under the other man's gaze, then crossed the veranda and was about to enter the post.

"Why don't you sit down?" the older man suggested. "I'll get whatever you want."

Calhoun halted, his leg throbbing viciously.

"You work here?"

"I own it. I'm Weymarn."

"Then maybe you can get me a hoe handle, Mr. Weymarn. This one's borrowed."

Weymarn nodded, swung a chair around and Calhoun, propping his crutch against the wall, gratefully slacked into it. He was sweating enormously, his every muscle trembling, and now he closed his eyes, waiting for his strength to come back. *I'm no damned good,* he thought wearily. *This'll take time.*

Presently Weymarn came out of the store with a hoe handle, leaned it against the wall, swung a chair around and settled into it. Calhoun declined his offer of a cigar, but Weymarn lighted up. Over the flare of the match Calhoun could see Weymarn watching him, observing his distress and helplessness. A faint anger stirred in Calhoun; he hoped it would come off better than this or else his plan was spoiled.

Weymarn said suddenly, "Didn't think you'd be in this kind of shape or I'd have called on you."

Calhoun looked at him curiously and Weymarn smiled faintly so that one of his mustaches lifted a little. "The lieutenant left in a hurry before I could talk with him much. I wanted to ask him how Maco broke out."

"He knifed the two troopers who were exercising him. The troopers were drunk and forgot to search him."

"You mean nobody laid a hand on him?"

"One of the troopers got in a shot and hit him. He didn't know where he hit him, but he thought it was the shoulder. We're sure it wasn't enough to stop him, though."

Weymarn nodded thoughtfully. "The lieutenant says the Army figures he'll head for the Big Salt Canyons."

Calhoun nodded. "He always does."

"That's too true," Weymarn agreed pleasantly.

He sat musing, drawing on his cigar, framing his next

question, when the sight of Trooper Ryan approaching the store apparently silenced him. The big Irishman's sling was already dirty and he was hatless Calhoun saw. As he approached, the ingrained surliness in the broad Irish face was plain.

Ryan was eying Calhoun now, and then he halted, standing in the street facing the veranda. "You never told me you got two meals last night," he said in a sullen voice.

Calhoun dipped his head. "Mine and yours."

"Why didn't you wake me?"

Calhoun eyed him with an amused tolerance. "If you'd been hungry you'd have been awake."

Ryan scowled. "The Army's paying for my food, but you're the one that gets it."

"Then stay awake," Calhoun said, irritable with pain.

Ryan was silent, his slow mind groping for a retort. Then, giving up, he mounted the steps and turned into the saloon.

Weymarn asked idly, "How are the Thompsons treating you?"

Calhoun's reply was laconic. "The food's good."

"Just the sight of Cap Thompson's face would spoil a meal for me," Weymarn observed.

Calhoun looked at him and, understanding, smiled faintly. "I know. What's his trouble?"

Weymarn grimaced in distaste. "He's just a shiftless blowhard, is all. He had a hard-scrabble outfit south of here until the 'Paches cleaned him out and killed his wife. He borrowed enough to start a teakettle lumber mill down by Silver City. Instead of hustling, he spent his time in the saloons blowing about how rich he'd be. All the time, his crew was stealing him blind—selling his logs and lumber and using his teams and wagons to deliver them and keeping the money. They cleaned him and he came back here with his tail between his legs. By that time his girl was old enough to work, so he retired."

Poor Hallie. No wonder she's Indian shy, Calhoun thought.

Weymarn went on, "He's got an old war wound he hides behind. I give him some harness to patch, but it's the girl who feeds them. Washes six days a week, bakes stuff to sell on the seventh."

As he ceased talking the sound of raised voices came from the bar. Calhoun saw Weymarn listen a moment and then, sensing trouble, rise, walk down the veranda and stand in the saloon door.

"What's the ruckus, Gus?" Weymarn demanded.

An angry voice came from the saloon's interior. "He's drunk a pint already and he wants more on credit. He's broke."

Weymarn said flatly, "Clear out of here, trooper! The lieutenant told me about you."

There was a long pause and then Ryan's surly voice came to Calhoun. "If it wasn't for us Army you'd all be dead. But ask for a little credit and you get thrown out."

"Go be a hero somewhere else," Weymarn said roughly; he stepped aside. Calhoun saw Ryan tramp through the door, an empty pint whisky bottle in his hand. Suddenly Ryan sailed the empty bottle out into the street and stood watching as it arced, fell and smashed. Calhoun knew that Ryan had drunk the pint of what was probably rotgut in only a matter of minutes and that soon it would explode inside of him. Weymarn probably knew this too, he guessed, which accounted for his ordering Ryan out.

Now Ryan swiveled his head and looked at Calhoun. Then he turned and came toward him on legs that were beginning to be unsteady. Weymarn followed two paces behind the trooper.

Abreast Calhoun, Ryan halted and Calhoun saw that his face was flushed with both whisky and quiet rage.

"They give you credit here because you're not Army?" Ryan demanded.

"I haven't asked for it."

"But you'll get it," Ryan said. "You'll get it like you got both our suppers."

Weymarn pulled up beside Ryan and put a hand on his shoulder. "That's enough of. . . ."

He never got to finish the sentence. Ryan whirled and sank a fist into Weymarn's belly and the force of the blow sent Weymarn jackknifing off the veranda and into the street on his back.

Calhoun was watching Weymarn so that he did not expect what followed. Ryan shifted his weight, then kicked out savagely at Calhoun's outstretched, hurt leg.

For a second Calhoun was sure he would faint from the purest agony. Immediately following he knew that he must get away from this berserk trooper. In pure panic he thrust himself by his arms out of the chair, wheeled on his one good leg and leaped for the wall, rolling his back against it. Ryan lunged for him and, acting by instinct, Calhoun swung the chair in front of the onrushing trooper. Ryan tripped and sprawled on his face and now Calhoun, his body raging with pain, knew that somehow he must fight. His hand touched his crutch-hoe and now he grasped it, shaking off the jacket padding and waited for Ryan to rise.

Out of the corner of his eye Calhoun saw Weymarn on hands and knees retching in the road.

Ryan was pushing to his knees now and then Calhoun said thinly, "Keep away from me, soldier, or I'll kill you."

Ryan stood erect now, swaying in his tracks, an ugly smile on his broad face. Then he made a lunge, not for Calhoun, but for the new hoe handle Weymarn had stood against the wall by the far chair. Seizing it, he faced Calhoun who, unable to move, was leaning against the wall, sparing his injured leg.

"I'll keep away from you all right," Ryan said. Then, using the hoe handle as a spear, he lunged at Calhoun who tried to parry the thrust and failed. The tip of the handle caught him in the chest and Ryan shoved. Calhoun grabbed for the wall logs, his fingers vainly raking for a hold, and then he toppled over backwards, the hoe still in his hand.

Calhoun knew bitterly that he was as helpless as a beetle

on its back. With a mighty effort he rolled over on his belly
and saw Ryan coming at him. Awkwardly then, he swung
the hoe blade first, like an ax, aiming it in an arc parallel to
the floor. The hoe blade caught Ryan behind the knee and
he shouted with pain and fell to his knees.

Calhoun saw Ryan in his drunken fury now raise the hoe
handle over his head with his one good hand and Calhoun
knew that Ryan would smash him through the veranda floor
if he could.

With a desperate crablike movement Calhoun raised on
his elbow, shortened his grip on the hoe handle and ran the
flat face of the hoe square in Ryan's face. The blow the
trooper started was never finished. He grunted with pain,
dropped his hoe handle and covered his smashed nose with
his good hand. The pain was so extreme that he fought to
get his hurt arm out of its sling so that he could raise his
other hand to his face.

Panting now, sweat streaming from his face, Calhoun
lengthened his grab on the hoe, and still belly down and on
an elbow brought the hoe back in a wide arc and swung the
back of the blade in a swift savage arc at Ryan's head. The
curved hook of the hoe caught Ryan behind the ear and
knocked him senseless against the wall. He hit it solidly,
then pitched on his face.

Calhoun collapsed then, his sweat-drenched face flat
against the post wall; his leg throbbed wildly and he was
dragging breath from the very bottom of his lungs. He lay
there for what seemed like minutes, then presently he heard
a voice above him, a woman's voice. "Sit there, Will. Are
you all right?"

"Yes, yes," Weymarn said impatiently. "Tend to him,
Belle."

Now the voice was closer and it spoke to him. "I'm going
to turn you over and put you in the chair. Say if it's all
right."

"All right," Calhoun whispered. He felt hands under his
arms and then he was slowly rolled over and lifted to a

sitting position. The woman was behind him and he could not see her face, nor did he want to. He was concentrating now on fighting the pain as she lifted him up and slid him into the barrel chair.

"Go get us a bottle, Belle," Weymarn said.

He heard the woman walk away down the veranda and slowly turned his head, not to look at her, but to observe Ryan who was sprawled out face down on the veranda.

"I hope you killed him," Weymarn observed. His face was white and Calhoun wondered if he looked as sick as the older man.

Now Calhoun heard the woman returning and he turned his head to look at her. With slow shock he knew immediately that he had known her many years ago, and he remembered the last place he'd seen her. She had been dealing faro in one of the better saloons in Silver City, one of the few women gamblers he'd run across and by far the best looking. She had been living with the saloon owner as his wife, but Calhoun had guessed that the "Mrs." before her acquired name was only to protect her from the attentions of the rough saloon crowd.

She was full-bodied and the blonde hair he remembered was now a true chestnut color and parted on the side. She could have been in her late thirties, a handsome woman with fair skin, an aquiline nose and green eyes that were now looking at the bottle of whisky from which she was trying to wrench the cork.

She succeeded as she halted in front of Calhoun, and as she extended the bottle she looked him squarely in the eyes.

"Calhoun, this is my wife," Weymarn said.

In the brief instant their glances met as Calhoun dipped his head in acknowledgment, he saw that she recognized him and was not going to acknowledge it.

"You're first, Mr. Calhoun." Calhoun accepted the bottle and took two deep shuddering drinks that lighted a fire inside him. Then he passed the bottle to Weymarn who tilted

it and drank deeply. Belle watched each man as he drank
and then she said to Weymarn, "Are you all right, Will?"

"I'm fine," Weymarn answered, handing back the bottle.
He looked over at Calhoun. "I think we'd better get you
back to your blankets."

Calhoun slowly shook his head. "No, I'm not going back
to Thompson's. I'd already made up my mind before Ryan
jumped me. If I went back now he'd bury a knife in me."
Now he looked directly at Weymarn. "Besides I'm broke. I
can't pay up, and I don't think the Army will pay for me."

Weymarn was frowning; he glanced quickly at Belle, then
back to Calhoun who went on doggedly, "Could you use a
man around your place here? If I can work to pay the
Thompsons for my meals, I can sleep anywhere."

Again Weymarn looked at Belle, and so did Calhoun. Was
she then the one who was to make the decision, Calhoun
wondered?

"Gus is leaving for Silver City this afternoon, remember?" Belle said. "You hate to tend bar, Will, and you know
it."

Weymarn nodded, almost reluctantly. "Our bartender
will be gone for a few days. Maybe you can spell him if you
want. I can't promise you anything beyond that, but we'll
see."

It was light that wakened Ryan in the middle of the night.
He opened his eyes, saw the lantern inches from his face and
instinctively he rolled away from it. Damn that Calhoun!
Then he remembered Calhoun had never returned and that
his saddle, rifle and blankets were gone. Only then did he
roll over to see Weymarn towering over him, watching him
with a faint amusement in his pale eyes. Now Weymarn
extended a pint bottle of whisky to him, remarking, "Don't
drink it all now. I want to talk with you."

Without hesitation Ryan reached for the whisky and sat
up. He didn't know what Weymarn wanted and after this

morning he didn't like him at all, but here was whisky, wonderful whisky.

Ryan took four deep swallows, feeling the sweet grasp of it, feeling it shock him awake. Tentatively he extended the bottle to Weymarn who said softly, "Keep it. How'd you like to be able to buy more of it?"

"Who wouldn't like it?" Ryan asked warily. The man wanted something, Ryan knew, or else he wouldn't be giving away whisky. Now, because the bottle was his own, he took another drink which added to the blessed warmth stealing over him.

"Fifty dollars will buy a lot of that stuff," Weymarn observed.

"That it will," Ryan said slowly. "What do I do for it?"

"Just ride over to the reservation with a message."

"Who for?"

"A young buck named Santiago. I don't know where you'll find him, but ask any of the young bucks. Not the old boys, the young bucks."

"What do I tell him?" Ryan asked curiously.

Weymarn was silent, his eyes watchful and secretive. Finally he said softly, "Tell him you can deliver Maco to him for fifty head of horses and a hundred head of cattle."

Ryan only stared at the older man while his slow mind took this in and then rejected it. "But I can't deliver Maco," he said finally.

Weymarn smiled faintly. "Yes, you can. Any time."

"You mean you got him?"

Weymarn did not answer either by word or gesture.

Now Ryan shifted his gaze and studied the bottle. Slowly caution built up in him. If the trip was as simple as this, why was he being sent as a messenger? Now he voiced his suspicion. "Why don't you ride over yourself?"

Weymarn shook his head. "Santiago knows me. He knows any man I'd send. If he traced the message back to me, I'd be in trouble. He doesn't know you, and he can't trace you to me."

"He'll know I'm Army."

"Not with the clothes I give you."

"I got a government-branded horse."

"You won't have. I'll give you a horse with a brand he won't know."

"What do I say to him?"

Weymarn thought a moment. "Tell him he's got five days after tomorrow's beef issue to get them to McNaughton's Springs. It's a two-day drive to Silver City from there. Tell him Maco will be freed as soon as the stock is in Silver City."

Ryan thought this over a long moment. "Fifty dollars, you say?"

"Twenty-five tonight. Twenty-five when you get back." He added, "That's a half-year's pay. It'll take you wherever you want to go."

"Go? My enlistment runs for. . . ." Then Ryan understood and smiled. "Desert, you mean?"

"I never knew a soldier with fifty dollars in his pocket who wouldn't desert if he got the chance. You've got three-weeks' head start on Benson."

Ryan grinned. "All right, you got yourself a messenger."

Weymarn said in a conversational voice, "I'm glad of that. Otherwise I'd have had to shoot you." He paused, letting this seep into Ryan's slow mind. Then he said briskly, "Get up. You're going tonight."

2

Next morning when Calhoun knocked at the Thompsons' back door, Hallie called to him to come in. He hobbled through the low doorway into the kitchen and immediately saw Cap seated at the round oilcloth-covered table in the middle of the room. Cap was cradling a cup of coffee in his hand and did not speak.

Calhoun nodded to him anyway, as he looked about the room. This was a poor room, he thought, holding only the barest necessities—a stove, a cupboard, table and chairs and in a corner a made-up cot. Beyond the kitchen was a single bedroom and Calhoun, looking at Cap, would have been willing to bet that the bedroom was his, the cot Hallie's.

Hallie, standing by the stove, was looking at him with puzzlement in her face. "We missed you yesterday," she said, and there was unconcealed reproof in her voice.

"I plain slept out the day," Calhoun said mildly. He hobbled over to the table, pulled out a chair, gingerly slacked into it and laid his crutch on the floor.

"If we fix meals for you and you don't show up, you pay for them," Cap said flatly.

"All right," Calhoun said mildly.

"Were you hurt again in the fight?" Hallie asked.

"Bruised, maybe," Calhoun said cheerfully.

Hallie crossed to the table with a steaming bowl of oatmeal and placed it before Calhoun. When she continued to stand there, he glanced up at her.

She said, "You didn't sleep in the shed last night."

"That's right. I've changed hotels."

"Dirt floor not good enough for you?" Cap asked angrily.

Calhoun continued to look at Hallie, ignoring Cap. "Lady, I'm broke," he said gently. "I've got me a cot in Weymarn's stable. No room rent. I've got a job in Weymarn's saloon starting today, so I can pay for my food if you want to feed me." Now he looked at Cap. "My friend, your worries are over. What I eat I'll pay for, so you can quit worrying about the Army."

He started to eat and Hallie slowly crossed the kitchen to dish up the meat and potatoes onto a granite-wear plate. She crossed back to the table with it, set it before Calhoun and poured his coffee.

"Is Ryan with you?" she asked.

Calhoun looked up at her and said drily, "That's not likely, after yesterday."

"He didn't sleep here either," Hallie said quietly. "His gun and blankets are gone."

Slowly Calhoun put down his fork. "Where did he go after the fight?"

Cap cut in in his sour voice, "One of Weymarn's men lugged him into the wash house. He slept off his drunk most of the day and we took supper out to him. His lamp was burning when I went to bed."

Calhoun shrugged and started to eat then. He had a fair idea of what had happened to Ryan. Without a commanding officer to check on him and with no troops to pursue him, Ryan had simply deserted. He would have three weeks head start on his pursuers, and in that time he could lose himself, change his name and be rid of his Army career. Calhoun didn't care if Ryan had deserted or not, but he could understand that Hallie, with Ryan's extra board money in sight, would be bitterly disappointed if his hunch was true. He decided not to voice his guess.

Cap suddenly sighed. "It looks like we come up with a pretty bad bargain, Hallie. Calhoun here gets free room and we lose the money. Now Ryan disappears."

"We're better off than we were," Hallie said quietly.

Cap rose now and said in a grumbling voice, "A man never has any luck." He started toward the door and Calhoun noticed that he had a slight limp. He wondered, since he hadn't noticed the limp before, if Cap was putting it on as an invitation to pity, a visible sign that he couldn't really work even if he wanted to.

Finished with his breakfast Calhoun picked up his hoe-handle crutch and rose.

Hallie said, "Weymarn will expect you to work through the noon hour. I'll send over a sandwich, like I do for Gus Henry. He's the bartender you're replacing."

"All right," Calhoun said. Starting across the room he caught sight of the rifle leaning against the open door. It reminded him of his last conversation with Hallie and he halted and pointed to it. "You know how to shoot that?"

Hallie flushed. "Not very well."

"Why not?"

"Shells for practice cost money, is why."

Calhoun could have bitten off his tongue. He said gruffly, "I'll bring you some powder and lead, and your father can load his own."

He stepped out into the morning and he felt a faint anger stirring within him. Cap Thompson was willing to leave Hallie alone a large part of the day and had never bothered to teach her to shoot. It was typical of the man, Calhoun knew; he'd probably never had an emotion or thought that didn't center on himself.

At the post Weymarn was standing in the open door of the store when Calhoun laboriously climbed the veranda steps. Weymarn shoved his big body away from the door-frame, paused and said, "I'll go round and open up. No use your coming through. How's the leg?"

Calhoun said it was all right and Weymarn disappeared inside the store. Calhoun moved up to the doorway and looked in. It was a big store, with counters running along either side and large tables in the middle. There was a hard-ware side, with lanterns, harness and pots hanging from the

ceiling, and kegs of bolts and nails stacked on the floor. The
middle tables were piled high with clothes, while the other
counter flanked the groceryside. Toward the rear, beside the
door that led into the barroom, there was a railed off space
holding a safe and desk.

When Calhoun heard the saloon door open he hobbled
over to it and stepped past Weymarn into the room. There
was a long solid painted lumber bar to his right, with an
unmatching and ornate back bar and mirror backing it up.
There were four round green-felt covered tables with chairs
that took up the rest of the room. Three kerosene overhead
lamps completed the sparse furnishings.

Weymarn led him behind the bar and Calhoun learned his
new trade in roughly ten minutes. Whisky came in two
grades and was sold by the shot or bottle. The price of cigars
and plug tobacco was marked on the boxes. There was a
short list of early-morning drinkers who were to be cut off at
two shots if they were to do a day's work.

New cards were stored under the bar so they couldn't be
tampered with. Since there was no house man to handle the
gambling, there was a straight rental of three dollars for the
use of the chips. No other markers were allowed. There
were four ax handles spotted along the shelf under the bar
for use in case of a roughhouse.

"Save all your bottles because we get our whisky by the
barrel," Weymarn concluded, and he pointed to a basket
under the bar, half full of empty bottles. "When that's full,
take it out and put it under the loading platform out back.
The door isn't locked."

That summed it up, and Weymarn went out the connecting door into the store as the first early-morning drinkers
started to trickle in for their rationed shots.

In an hour the saloon was empty and Calhoun came out
from behind the bar and gratefully lowered himself in a
chair. His leg was throbbing already and there was a long
day ahead of him.

He heard footsteps behind him and, thinking a customer

had come through the rear door from the post, he reached for his hoe handle and began to rise.

"Don't get up," a woman's pleasant voice said. Without turning, Calhoun knew it was Belle Weymarn.

She came from behind him, rounded the table, and pulled out a chair. She was wearing a long-sleeved blue dress with a canvas storekeeper's apron over it, and, still standing, she untied the apron strings and removed the apron, saying, "I hate that thing, but it does save dresses."

Calhoun knew he must have looked puzzled because she explained, "I clerk in the store."

She sat down facing him, folded her arms on the table and carefully regarded him, a faint beginning smile on her face.

Calhoun asked quietly, "Am I supposed not to know you?"

"Do you know me?"

Calhoun nodded.

"I think we better pretend we met for the first time yesterday."

Again Calhoun nodded, accepting this, but he wondered if the contempt he felt for her showed in his eyes.

Now she smiled openly. "It's not what you think. Will knows I lived with Johnson. I never lied to him because I couldn't. He met me in the Happy Day." She paused and said soberly, "It's just that he hates it when a man comes by who knew me before we were married."

"He's jealous, maybe?"

She looked at him appraisingly and then smiled. "That's a nice compliment, even if you didn't intend it to be." She added, "Yes, I suppose he is a little jealous."

She was, Calhoun decided, a handsome woman. Only the barest noticeable tension at the corners of her mouth and a kind of sad wisdom in her eyes gave a hint of the past.

"As I recall it you were dealing faro when I was freighting into Silver City. One week you were there, the next week you'd gone."

Belle nodded and grimaced faintly. "It was only a stunt

that Johnson thought up. Women aren't really good gamblers and it cost Johnson a lot to prove it."

"He still in Silver City?" Calhoun asked.

Belle smiled faintly. "Yes. And if you're wondering if I divorced him, the answer is that I was never married to him. I'll even answer another question you're too polite to ask. I *am* married to Will."

"His idea or yours?" Calhoun asked, openly curious now.

"His," Belle said quietly. "He took me away from Johnson because there was nothing keeping me there. He didn't want that to happen with him."

Calhoun observed, "I don't think anything would keep you if you decided this wasn't for you."

"You're wrong," Belle said. "You've heard there's no liquor hater like the reformed drunkard. Well, marriage always looks best to the woman who's never been offered it. Even marriage to Will Weymarn."

"Even?" Calhoun repeated.

Belle moved her hand in a gesture that included the room. "This isn't very exciting," she said reflectively. "Selling lollypops to kids and trade goods to Apaches when they're not too scared to come in. Every day like the next, and with no real friends to help out. Still, it's all something you can count on, like I can count on Will. It may not be much, but it's here."

Calhoun was puzzled. Twice she had spoken of Weymarn slightingly, and Calhoun wondered what their real relations were. He said mildly, "You sound like a man who's made a bad contract, but not so bad that he'll risk being sued and lose everything he has, if he breaks it."

"You mean what I say about Will?"

Calhoun nodded.

"It's queer you should use the word contract," Belle said quietly. "That's just what it was. He was lonesome and needed a woman. I wasn't young and my looks were going. He owned the store, saloon, mill, a ranch and a freighting outfit." She paused. "That's a fair enough trade, isn't it?"

Calhoun nodded. "You can do without the frosting if you have the cake."

"You mean I can do without the butter if I have the bread," Belle said, a faint irony in her tone. "Will's hard and he doesn't mind stomping on people when he needs to. He's in love with money and sometimes I think money is in love with him. But he's been kind enough to me, another man's woman."

The clatter of horses hoofs and the sound of jingling harness came from the street, interrupting their conversation. Calhoun turned his head and saw the stage pull up in the street; the hostler was already unhitching for the team exchange. The driver swung down and then the first passengers drifted into the bar. One was an Army captain who pulled off his hat and, standing in the doorway, beat out the dust that had settled in every wrinkle of his blue uniform.

The other man, big and bearded and dressed in newly washed range clothes, halted to let the sun glare wash out of his eyes. He saw Belle and Calhoun then and slowly tramped over to them.

Calhoun rose and was reaching for his crutch as the stranger said, "Never thought I'd find girls at this crossroads crib. Let me buy you a drink, honey."

Calhoun pulled himself erect and said thinly, "Don't you see the wedding ring, you fool?"

The bearded man only looked at him in amiable puzzlement. "So she wears a ring," he conceded. "Then what's she doing sitting in a saloon waiting to sucker the stage passengers?" He turned to Belle. "Come on, honey, let's drink up."

Belle rose and started to turn when the bearded man reached out and seized her arm.

Calhoun swung for the beard then and connected solidly. The big man staggered back a step, caught his balance, then lunged for Calhoun, both arms windmilling. Calhoun caught the second blow on the chest, lost his precarious balance and fell sprawling on his back at Belle's feet.

He rolled over onto his good knee, his other leg straight behind him and tried to push himself erect and could not.

At that moment Belle reached down, palmed the gun out of his holster, cocked it and pointed it at the bearded man. "Go pick up that hoe handle and give it to him!" she said in a hard voice.

The bearded traveler stared at her in amazement and then, seeing she was serious, he went over to the hoe handle and picked it up.

Calhoun, still on his knee, accepted the crutch and pulled himself erect.

Belle said now, in the same hard voice, "Now go get in that stage, you flannel-mouthed son of a bitch! If you stick your head out of it, I'll shoot!"

Meekly the bearded man turned, tramped past the captain who had witnessed this in silence, and climbed docilely into the stage.

Calhoun reached out for the pistol and looked at Belle Weymarn, both embarrassment and pity in his eyes.

"He knew," she said softly, bitterly. "You see it doesn't wash off."

He watched her pick up her apron, her face still and cold and move on through the door to the post. She'd made her bargain with life, Calhoun thought, but it was as she said, it was an imperfect bargain. The respectability she had traded for was so transparent that a transient saloon bum saw through it. She was, Calhoun reflected, a tough, good and honest woman.

Now he heard the coin rap on the counter, followed by the captain's voice, "I'd like a drink before that stage leaves if I can get it."

A little before noon, when there was not a customer in the saloon, Sam Avery stepped through the veranda door. He was carrying something in a clean towel and set it on the bar top, saying, "Hallie's special."

"You've spent a lot of time waiting on me," Calhoun said

mildly. He looked under the towel and saw some bacon sandwiches. Gesturing toward them he said, "Help yourself."

"No. She's fixing mine now," Sam said.

Calhoun lifted out a sandwich and bit into it, studying the man before him. All he knew about him was that he occasionally helped Hallie. He was a pleasant enough looking man, slow talking, deliberate in his movements, and he had big work-roughened hands and wore clean worn range clothes and half boots.

"You board with the Thompsons, Sam?"

Avery nodded soberly. "Ever since Hallie started. More now than I used to, though. I used to have a pretty steady lumber freighting job, but since this 'Pache scare we don't move much. We wait until they got enough lumber cut for five, six wagons and then we travel together. Only makes a couple of days' work in two weeks."

"When did Hallie start?" Calhoun asked.

"When she was fifteen."

"Cap been laid up that long?"

"No. He got worse after we got engaged."

Calhoun hoped the surprise didn't show in his face. Hallie engaged to this man was something Calhoun found it hard to comprehend. There was nothing wrong with him except that he was fifteen years older than Hallie, probably a slow plodder who was not even astute enough to know that Cap was shamming and who was not observant enough to realize that Cap imposed unmercifully on Hallie.

"When do you and Hallie get married?" Calhoun asked.

"Oh, there's no hurry," Sam said slowly. "We'll wait until times get a little better for us both."

Calhoun said nothing, but he thought grimly *They'll never get better for you, Sam.*

"How's the new job?" Sam asked.

"Nothing to it."

"Well, I better get back to dinner."

As he was turning away from the bar, Calhoun said quietly, "Stay around her as much as you can, Sam."

Avery halted and looked at him in puzzlement, his mouth open a little. "What for?"

"She's scared."

"Indians?"

Calhoun nodded and Sam stared at him thoughtfully. "She never said anything to me about it."

"She probably doesn't want to worry you," Calhoun said mildly. "When I'm scared, I don't want anybody to know." He smiled and now Sam nodded as if he agreed and smiled.

"I'll do that."

Calhoun thanked him for bringing the sandwiches and watched him go out. There was something wrong about a man who didn't know his girl was scared and there was something strange about a girl who wouldn't tell her man. Come to think of it, there was something wrong about a man who would say there was no hurry about marrying Hallie. And there was also something queer about a girl who, if she loved a man enough to become engaged to him, wouldn't ask him to take her out of the mean and drab surroundings she was living in.

Calhoun began to rinse and wipe the glasses. The thing he couldn't understand was that Hallie had never mentioned her engagement. But why should she? he thought then. He was simply a new boarder, a stranger whom she must tolerate for money and had no claim to any part of her private life. A half-forgotten midnight confidence didn't even entitle him to worry about her, so he wouldn't.

It was mid-afternoon when the first card players drifted in and from then on Calhoun was busy. By suppertime he was almost too busy, and he wondered when Weymarn would relieve him. However, help never came; Weymarn was probably so used to letting his bartender run the saloon that he never thought of it, Calhoun decided. He sent a friendly customer into the store for crackers and a can of peaches and ate his supper in snatches and standing up.

Around ten o'clock the card games broke up and the more sober of the patrons scattered to their beds. Calhoun leaned against the back bar, dead beat from this full day that he had spent on one leg. A couple of teamsters were arguing mildly at the head of the bar. They had bought a bottle so he had nothing to worry about.

It was then Weymarn stepped into the bar from the store. He nodded to Calhoun, then opened the cupboard doors under the back bar, took out two gallon jugs of the cheapest whisky and disappeared into the store.

Calhoun yawned, only mildly curious. The two teamsters tossed off their last drink, said good night and now Calhoun moved up to the front doors, locked them, pulled down the overhanging kerosene lamp, blew it and made his way down the barroom in the dark. I'll clean up in the morning, he thought.

As he passed through the door into the store he saw Weymarn waiting on a customer under the only lamp that was still lighted. The customer was an Apache squaw and Weymarn, with a trader's patience, was leaning against the back counter, arms folded. Calhoun smiled faintly. The squaw had probably been here all afternoon and evening debating on how best to spend her few coins. Calhoun waved to Weymarn and then hobbled out through the back door onto the big loading platform where he paused to let his eyes adjust to the pitch black of the night. He was waiting motionless when he heard the stomp of horses' hoofs and the soft jingle of harness. Presently his eyes accustomed themselves to the darkness and he made out the shape of a team and buckboard. The Apache squaw's, he wondered?

Now he moved toward the steps, slowly descended them and halted at the bottom to let the pain in his leg ease off. For no reason at all he was remembering Weymarn's curious visit to the bar and his exit with two gallons of whisky. Immediately afterwards, Calhoun had closed the bar, then found the lone customer in the store was the Apache squaw. Was there a connection, he wondered?

Glancing at the rear door, he saw the thin crack of light under it, and then he moved toward the buckboard. Halting beside it, he fumbled in its bed. There were some canned goods that he recognized by touch and then his hand moved beyond toward a blanket. Immediately he knew, feeling the hard round shapes that here were the two jugs of whisky.

For a moment Calhoun stood still in the night taking this in. His employer, then, was selling whisky to the Indians. Two gallons of whisky in the stomachs of a dozen wild young bucks could start a burning and killing raid that would sweep for a hundred miles. And Weymarn was willing to risk this for the twenty-five dollars the two gallons probably brought him. What had Belle said, *He's in love with money and sometimes I think money is in love with him.*

Calhoun's lip curled in contempt as he thought of this. Weymarn's Crossing itself might be raided and Weymarn himself killed, but the greed in the man made him blind to his own risk. Well, the whisky wouldn't be delivered, Calhoun decided. He reached in and lifted out both jugs. It was impossible for him to hold a jug in the crutch hand, so he unbuckled his belt, threaded it through the jug handle and tightened his belt. Then, with the second jug in his free hand, he hobbled past the blacksmith's shop and corral to the log stable.

He didn't know if the squaw would check to see if her whisky was there when she came out. If so she would demand another two gallons from Weymarn. But if she trusted Weymarn and had seen him take the whisky out, she might assume the jugs were in the buckboard. Either way she'd get the whisky eventually, Calhoun knew, but at least he was doing all he could.

As soon as Hallie had climbed between the blankets on her kitchen cot, Cap Thompson blew out the lamp and stepped out into the pleasant star-shot night. He wasn't sleepy and since he'd done nothing today except play pinochle all afternoon with old Bailey Harris, he wasn't tired.

Late this afternoon Weymarn had given him some harness to mend and, figuring he might as well work on it for a while, he turned toward the wash shed.

Inside, he lighted the lantern, lifted the empty tubs off the table, threw the harness on it and then picked up his awl, hammer, knife and can of rivets from one of the several wall shelves. Seating himself, he began to work, and while his hands were working his mind wandered elsewhere. He was remembering how upset Hallie had been tonight when Calhoun, as before, hadn't showed up for supper. This morning Calhoun had agreed to pay for the meals he'd missed, and Cap would see to it that he paid for this one. It was a pity that he and Hallie needed the money so badly, or he would have told Calhoun not to come around any more. Thinking of the man, Cap grew halfway angry. There was a sleepy indifference about the man that trapped you into wanting to stir him up; when you succeeded it drew a biting, quietly savage response that made you hate the man.

A dog began to bark out in the night and Cap heard a horse approaching. It halted, there was a creak of saddle leather and then a man stepped into the doorway still holding the reins of his horse. He was a tall, unshaven young man in dirty range clothes and muddy halfboots; sleeplessness stained the skin under his eyes and slacked his simple, ordinary and unshaven face. He was no sooner in the door than he looked out uneasily into the night.

Cap said, "Come for your wash, Wilkie?"

Wilkie Brown nodded and Cap rose. On the shelf behind him were several bundles of clothes and Cap hesitated only a moment before he lifted out the bundle tied with the red bandanna. He put it on the table before Wilkie and then looked at him. It came to Cap almost with shock that he was looking into the face of a frightened man. He said, curiously, "What's the matter with you?"

Wilkie Brown licked his lips. "You haven't got a bottle I could buy off you, have you, Cap? The saloon and the store are both closed."

"Up at the house I have."

"Get it. I'll pay you."

Cap stepped past him and his horse, went up to the house, felt his way across to the kitchen cupboard, took out a bottle and a glass and tiptoed out. He could hear Hallie's quiet, regular breathing and he knew he had not wakened her. Turning back to the shed, Cap wondered what was wrong with Wilkie. He remembered him looking over his shoulder into the night and he thought, remembering Wilkie's reputation as a woman chaser, *Somebody's brother is likely after him.*

In the shed he put the bottle and glass in front of Wilkie who was seated on the edge of the table. Wilkie uncorked the bottle and poured several fingers of raw whisky into the glass. Cap noticed that the bottle was beating a small tattoo on the rim of the glass.

"You must have ridden a long ways," Cap said drily. "You're shaking."

Almost mechanically Wilkie lifted the glass and drained it. After wiping his mouth on the back of his hand, he said, "For a fact." Then he added, "This here light looked awfully good to me."

"You scared of the dark?" Cap asked derisively.

"Nowadays, yes." Wilkie poured himself another drink and Cap watched him, contempt mounting in his eyes.

"Then you don't know a damned thing about Apaches, Wilkie. A man's always safe at night with them. They won't fight at night."

"You willing to guarantee that?" Wilkie asked.

"You think you're being followed?"

"I might be." Wilkie's voice was almost a whisper.

"Talk up!" Cap said almost angrily. "Who's following you?"

Wilkie only shook his head.

"Well, where you been, then, you're so scared?"

"I can't tell you."

"Why not?" Cap demanded.

"It's a secret," Wilkie said, almost angrily. "I'd get shot if I opened my mouth."

"Who'd shoot you?" Cap scoffed.

"Never mind, never mind," Wilkie said curtly.

Cap laughed unpleasantly then. "You'd make a hell of a rider, Wilkie. You'd spook any cow that came within a hundred yards of you. You smell scared. I'm surprised your horse didn't pitch you."

"Who said I was working cattle?" Wilkie asked. There was a slyness in his voice as he reached out for the bottle and poured a wicked drink.

As he slugged it down, Cap said, "Well, you're drawing punchers' wages."

"Not anymore I ain't," Wilkie said flatly, his voice beginning to thicken.

"Sure, you look like a man with a big stake," Cap jeered.

Wilkie's simple face flushed in anger and he said harshly, "I got a stake, don't you worry. You draw more'n riders' wages for risking your neck night and day for a week, for eating cold grub, for not smoking, for standing night guard with all the time wondering when them murdering Apaches will hit you. You get real money for that."

On the heel of his tirade he reached in his pocket, drew out his fist and threw five silver dollars on the table in front of Cap. "That's for the wash and the drinks," Wilkie said angrily. "Ask the other Weymarn punchers if they can pay off like that." He picked up his wash, jammed it under his arm and went out, ignoring all the amenities in his anger.

Slowly Cap reached out and picked up the silver dollars. Wilkie, he decided, must have a stake if he could throw money away like that. He just wasn't that drunk.

Cap leaned back in his chair and put his attention to this. Wilkie had been genuinely afraid and he'd come off a job that was so secret he was afraid of being shot if he disclosed what it was. He'd been on this job a week and had been paid well for risking his neck, eating cold grub, not smoking and for standing night guard. What did it all add up to?

Cap puzzled over each item separately, then put them together, but they still told him nothing. It sounded to him as if Wilkie might have been running whisky to the Indians.

Wilkie knew he was a little drunk when he rode out of Cap's yard and his fear had been replaced by anger. The old fool had baited him into throwing away good money just to prove he was making a stake. Well, there'd be plenty more coming from the same place and he supposed he could afford it.

Maybe there'd been no reason for his fear, but Wilkie hadn't been without it since Weymarn assigned him and Ollie Matson to the job of guarding Maco. True, Maco was down a wet, ladderless, twenty-foot abandoned mine shaft. It was also true Maco understood that if he even raised his voice he would be shot. Still the Apaches were on the hunt for him and they were beating the country. Yesterday Wilkie had laid on his belly in the brush only a hundred yards from the mine shaft and had watched the Apaches pass by only a hundred feet below. If Maco had yelled at that moment Wilkie would be a dead man. Even now they or some other Apaches might yet cut the trail of his horse and follow it back to the mine shaft. He was desperately thankful that luck had been with him when he and Ollie had tossed a coin to see who would come into the Crossing to replenish their provisions.

He cut down the alley beside the store and rode in the darkness toward the corral where he dismounted and in putting down his bundle of laundry, found his legs a little unsteady. He wasn't really drunk, he thought; he'd just taken the stuff too fast.

After unsaddling and turning his horse into the corral, he headed for the stable and saw that there was a lantern lighted inside. Gently lurching down the centerway, he halted in front of the stall where the lantern was hanging on a wall nail. A man he didn't know was lying on a cot in a corner.

Wilkie hauled up, scowling at the stranger's presence. "You working for Weymarn?"

The stranger nodded. "I'm relieving the bartender. Name's Calhoun."

"Mine's Wilkie Brown." That was all right then, Wilkie thought. He noticed now that he was seeing two of the lanterns and he shook his head to bring the twin images into focus before he threw his laundry on the floor, moved on down the dark centerway and found the loft ladder. Climbing it, he found the two folded blankets he kept here for his town trips, descended and made his unsteady way back to the stall. Uninvited, he threw his blankets on the floor next to his laundry, sat down and leaned back against the wall. Now he saw the hoe handle lying beside Calhoun's cot and he frowned drunkenly.

"What's that?" He pointed to the hoe handle.

"I use it for a crutch."

"Hell, if you're crippled you can do better than that," Wilkie said thickly.

"I won't be crippled long enough to bother."

Again Wilkie was seeing two of everything. He closed his eyes a moment and then wondered what he'd been talking about with this man. Oh, yes, a cripple.

Opening his eyes, he asked, "Horse throw you?"

"I got an Apache lance in my leg."

"Hurts, huh?" Wilkie said thickly. And now his interest was aroused. "When was this?"

"I was guiding a patrol that was after Maco. We got jumped."

"Maco," Wilkie stupidly repeated after him. Oh, the things he could tell this crippled bartender, Wilkie thought. Immediately then came a caution. Not a word about Maco. The best thing to do was to pretend total ignorance of everything that had happened, so he said, "I thought he was in the guardhouse at Fort Kelso."

"Not any more."

Wilkie pretended indifference. He reached for a sack of

tobacco and clumsily rolled a crooked cigarette which sifted tobacco out its end as he wiped a match alight. He could not concentrate on the flame, but as he tried his glance lifted above the flame to the two jugs under the cot. "What's in them?" he said, pointing with the match.

"Whisky."

Wilkie threw the match and the cigarette away. "Yours?"

"No."

Wilkie stared at him resentfully. If he could only get another drink maybe it would clear his head. "You figure anybody will miss a bite out of one?" he asked.

"Not just one bite," Calhoun said. "Go ahead."

Wilkie rose, staggered, caught himself, went over to the cot, knelt and pulled out the jug. Uncorking it, he took four shuddering swallows before his stomach started to buck. When he had his breath, he said, "Much obliged," and lurched over to his blankets and sat down.

This was better, Wilkie decided. The shock of the whisky had jarred him awake. Now he tried to remember what they'd been talking about. Maco, that was it. Maco had escaped and this bartender had been guiding the troops who were after him. Well, he'd pretend he didn't know anything about Maco's escape. That was the safest way to play it.

"You say Maco got out. How?"

He listened slyly as Calhoun said, "A couple of drunk troopers were exercising him. He'd hid a knife in his legging. At the end of the beat they were walking he knifed them both and ran."

Right straight to Weymarn, Wilkie thought smugly; right to him instead of the reservation where the Army thought he'd go; right to where he hoped Weymarn, who had sold him whisky and guns in the past, would feed and shelter him until he was well. Wilkie wanted to smile, but he was careful about that. But as long as he gave nothing away he might as well tease this Calhoun, he thought. "You figure the Army will get him?" he asked.

"No."

"Didn't they catch him once before?"

"He trusted the older people and they told the Army where he was. This time he won't trust them."

Calhoun's voice was getting fainter and now Wilkie knew he was drunk and that he couldn't fight off sleep much longer. He said in a slurred voice, "Mind if I turn that lantern down?"

"Turn it out if you want."

Wilkie rose and lurched across the room to the lantern and blew it.

With the light gone, it was better. Wilkie staggered back to his blankets, trying to remember what they'd been talking about. In a few seconds it came to him, and now he knelt down and pawed out his blankets. "You figure Maco will head for Mexico?"

Calhoun's voice came from a distance. "I think he's there now."

Wilkie smiled openly now, because it was dark and Calhoun couldn't see him; he said sleepily, "If he can walk or ride as far as Mexico with them bullet holes in his leg, I'll be surprised." He was drowning in drunken sleep and welcomed it.

Wilkie Brown's last words ran through Calhoun's mind and as he stared wide-eyed into the darkness, he tried to recall them. *If he can walk or ride as far as Mexico with them bullet holes in his leg, I'll be surprised,* this drunken puncher had said.

How did Brown know Maco was wounded, and why did he mention the bullet holes in his leg when both troopers thought they hit Maco in the shoulder?

Instantly, Calhoun rolled off the cot, reached for the still warm lantern, lighted it, picked up his crutch and hobbled over to Wilkie, who was lying face to the wall, breathing deeply. Kneeling beside him, Calhoun put a hand on his shoulder and shook him. Brown's slack body gave under Calhoun's hand. Roughly then, Calhoun shook him again, but Wilkie did not rouse.

Cursing softly Calhoun withdrew his hand. He knew that nothing short of throwing Brown into the water trough outside would awaken him from his drunken sleep.

Calhoun went back to his cot, blew the lantern and rolled into his blankets. He would see Brown in the morning. Right now Calhoun had his choice of believing one of two things. The first was that Wilkie Brown had already heard of Maco's escape and out of some perverse sense of humor was pretending he hadn't.

The second was that *Wilkie Brown had seen Maco.*

At bare daybreak Calhoun was roused from sleep by the distant barking of dogs. Immediately, remembering last night, he raised up on an elbow and saw that Wilkie Brown was not in his blankets. Lifting the hoe handle, he pulled himself to his feet, put on his hat and hobbled out into the runway. Looking through the double doors, he saw a man working inside the corral and as he moved out into the early morning light he saw that it was Brown saddling his horse.

Hobbling across the stable lot, Calhoun noted without thinking about it that the dogs still kept up their insane yammering. Letting himself into the corral, Calhoun lurched over to where Brown was cinching up, and now he saw his own big chestnut leave the bunch on the far side of the corral and come toward him.

Wilkie turned at the sound of his approach and grinned in a friendly way. "Nice day," he observed.

Calhoun studied him closely, wondering if the man remembered anything of last night's happenings. Calhoun's chestnut came up now and as he scratched the big gelding's neck, he decided not to push Brown.

"How're you feeling?"

"A little head soaking fixed me up this morning," Wilkie said cheerfully.

"Taking off this morning?" Calhoun asked idly.

"I'm packing some grub out to the ranch as soon as the store opens."

"Remember what you told me last night?" Calhoun asked without challenge.

Wilkie turned to look at him and now his eyes were alert and wary. "Every word of it," he said shortly.

"About Maco?"

"What about him?"

Calhoun thought he detected a faint note of caution in the question.

"About how bad he's hurt in the leg," Calhoun said.

"Who said he was?"

"You did."

Wilkie scowled. "Everyone knows that."

Calhoun said in mock puzzlement, "But I thought you said you didn't know he'd broken loose."

Now Wilkie smiled. "I guess you fell for that, didn't you? I was having some fun with you."

Calhoun smiled faintly now. "I reckon you had your fun."

"You've told that story so many times to so many people I kind of felt left out. I wanted to hear it from you."

Calhoun felt a faint embarrassment. It was true that he had told the story of Maco's escape so many times that he was sick of repeating it.

"You figure there's a man in this country that don't know the story?" Wilkie demanded.

"I suppose not. I hadn't heard that Maco was shot in the leg, though."

Wilkie laughed. "I've heard he was shot in the heel, the butt, the right arm and the head. Seems like everybody that tells the story shoots him in a different place."

"Sure," Calhoun said easily. "I heard it was in the arm myself." He did not want to alarm Wilkie and he knew the best way to avoid this was to seem to believe his story. Now he slapped his chestnut on the rump and said, "Get along, boy."

To Wilkie he said, "Well, I've got the bar to sweep out before breakfast. I'd better get at it."

Lurching on his crutch toward the gate, Calhoun felt a faint excitement stirring within him. Everything Wilkie had said was plausible, yet there had been an initial wariness that indicated Wilkie might have something to hide. But, supposing he did have something to hide, where could he have seen Maco? Had he talked with some Apaches who had seen him or was he, as he had said, simply repeating rumors that were as common as dirt? Calhoun didn't know, but it bothered him not to know.

Opening the gate and stepping through it, Calhoun was aware again of the barking of dogs and he wondered if they had something treed. His horse had followed him across the corral and now Calhoun gave him a parting slap on the neck. Looking over his horse, he saw Trooper Ryan's mount, with its U. S. brand, slowly start toward him and then stop. Calhoun knew that his and Ryan's horses, being strangers to the rest of the bunch, were probably not accepted by the others yet.

Turning toward the saloon, he remembered that the key Weymarn had given him was for the front door and he began the circle of the big building. The dogs, he noted, were still barking. As he came up to the front of the building and turned past the veranda, he halted, puzzlement coming into his face. Standing in the middle of the street, their heads pointed toward the post, were three dogs.

Their hackles were up and two were barking savagely while the third lifted his muzzle to the morning sky in a wild howl. Slowly, cursing softly, Calhoun limped out toward the dogs. They looked at him, then looked back at the post and continued their barking. Calhoun approached them, balanced on one leg, and slashed at them with the hoe handle. They easily avoided his blows, but two of them did not cease their barking. The other dog whined anxiously and wagged his tail at Calhoun when he said, "What the hell's the matter with you boys?"

Turning, Calhoun hobbled toward the steps and concentrated on pulling himself up to the veranda. He was on it, facing the post door when he saw the object lying against the doorsill. For a stunned moment there was puzzlement in Calhoun's face, and then he understood.

The object was wrapped in dirty cloth; it was a severed man's arm holding a silver dollar in its unclenched fist. It was Ryan's arm and, so that no one could mistake it, it had been wrapped in the sling Ryan had worn.

3

Calhoun stood utterly still, and he felt his stomach churn. He turned his back to the sight then and for a moment the shock of it held him witless. Then the questions, all of them unanswerable, flooded into his mind. Where had Ryan gone? Why had he been murdered? What was the significance of the silver dollar in the palm of the hand? Why had the arm been left at the trading-post door?

The insane barking of the dogs started up again. Calhoun hobbled down the steps and, cursing softly, picked up a handful of stones and threw them savagely at the dogs. They broke and ran, then halted far down the road to watch him.

Turning now, Calhoun hobbled around the corner of the veranda to the steps leading up the side of the building to the Weymarns' rooms over the post. Halting, he called "Weymarn!" and beat on the steps with his crutch. He called again and now Weymarn, gray hair tousled and in the act of tucking his shirt tail into his trousers, appeared on the landing.

"You'd better come down here," Calhoun called.

Something in his voice made Weymarn ask, "Trouble?" as he started down the stairs.

Calhoun didn't bother to answer. He turned and hobbled ahead of Weymarn toward the veranda steps, mounted, looked at the older man and dipped his head toward the arm.

Weymarn, a scowl of puzzlement on his face, climbed the last step, took two slow steps toward the door and then halted so abruptly that he might have walked into a wall. He, too, was motionless for seconds and then his big head turned toward Calhoun. His pale eyes held sober shock.

"Ryan?"

Calhoun nodded. "Sling and all."

Now the older man looked back at the arm, revulsion in his face. "Why did the damned Indians leave it here?" he asked angrily.

"Why did they kill him in the first place?" Calhoun countered.

Weymarn's expression was thoughtful, then he said slowly, tentatively, "Well, he was Army."

Calhoun gestured toward the arm. "How did they know he was? Look at that rolled-up shirt sleeve. That's not Army issue."

Weymarn nodded in silent agreement. "The brand on his horse then," he suggested.

"His horse is in the corral."

Again Weymarn nodded agreement. "So it is, I'd forgotten."

"What could the silver dollar mean?"

Weymarn's thick shoulders lifted in a shrug and he sighed. "Son, you're asking questions I wish I could answer."

Carefully watching the older man's face now, Calhoun asked matter-of-factly, "Was Ryan working for you?"

The big head swiveled around and the look of amazed protest was on his face. "Working for me? Why, you saw me throw him out of my saloon."

If Weymarn was lying, he was a good actor, Calhoun thought. Still, anyone who would sell whisky to Apaches was capable of lying. Calhoun came back to Weymarn's original question. "Then why did they leave it here?"

"Well, I guess they wouldn't leave it anywhere else," Weymarn's tone of voice was reasonable. "All the people here and for miles around come to the store. I'd guess it's a warning of what might be coming."

"The Apaches don't warn," Calhoun said quietly.

Both men heard the footsteps at the same time and turned. One of Weymarn's teamsters was crossing the road, heading for the veranda steps and the saloon. Weymarn looked at Calhoun and sighed. "Too late now."

When Calhoun only looked puzzled, Weymarn said, "We should've hid it. The whole place will be shooting at every shadow."

Now the teamster nodded a good morning and started up the steps.

"Bates, get a shovel and bury that thing." Weymarn nodded his head toward the arm. The teamster mounted the steps, looked at the arm, then halted as abruptly as Weymarn had. His mouth sagged open and he looked swiftly at Weymarn.

"Bu—bury it?" he stammered.

Weymarn reached in his pocket and brought out a set of keys on a ring from which he singled out one. "Go back into the storeroom. There's an old ground sheet lying on some new rope in the back corner. Bring it back and wrap that up in it." He extended the keys.

Bates accepted them and started toward the door, gingerly skirting the arm. Now he halted and looked at Weymarn. "That's that redheaded soldier's," he said.

Weymarn only nodded and now Bates inserted the keys in the lock and opened the door.

"Wait!" Weymarn said sharply; it was almost a shout. "I said get the shovel! I'll get the tarp."

He was moving as he spoke and now Bates stood aside and let him pass.

Weymarn's sudden sharp command and his haste as he went into the store struck both men as being so strange that they watched Weymarn disappear before they looked at each other.

"He afraid I'll steal something?" Bates growled as he passed Calhoun to descend the veranda steps and turn toward the back of the building.

Calhoun stood motionless, briefly puzzled at Weymarn's sudden anger. And then he heard voices in the street. Turning he saw a pair of early-morning drinkers headed for the saloon. Slowly then he moved, giving the grisly arm one last look, hobbled down to the saloon door and opened it. Putting a bottle and two shot glasses on the counter, he went to the rear of the saloon, got the broom and started his sweeping chore.

As he clumsily worked at pushing the broom, he was thinking, Something's wrong here. What memory, thought or decision was it that had triggered off Weymarn's sudden command to Bates? In effect it was an order to keep out of the storeroom. Why had Ryan's arm been left on the veranda unless it held a special message? *To Weymarn,* he wondered? If the Apaches had wanted Ryan's murder to be known, all they needed to do was leave the body on any trail or road to be discovered by the first passer-by. And what was the meaning of the silver dollar in the palm?

Calhoun had seen many senseless killings by Apaches, but this was not one of them. There was a reason for this one.

Now the first early-morning drinkers, talking excitedly, came into the saloon and Calhoun knew he had missed another breakfast.

Cap Thompson had finished a leisurely breakfast and noting the time said, "Calhoun's late."

"I know," Hallie said.

Cap rose now. "Well, give him ten more minutes and then

quit. Tell him he's just missed another meal that he'll pay for." At Hallie's nod, he asked, "Can you let me finish that piece of harness before you start washing?"

"All right, Dad."

"I'll fire up." He stepped out into the still cool morning, patted the dog and then headed for the wash house. He had built the fire and was working deftly on the harness when Hallie stepped through the doorway. She had changed into her short-sleeved working dress of a gray material that held soap and water stains, and as she crossed the room to get the buckets that she would fill at the creek, she observed, "Something must have happened, Dad. All the men in town seem to be collecting at the post."

Cap frowned. "Wonder what that could be? I'd better go see."

Throwing the harness in a corner, he lifted the tubs back onto the table and then stepped out into the morning, a faint excitement touching him. Only big news could have kept everybody away from their work at this hour. When he reached the corner of the house and looked upstreet, what he saw confirmed what Hallie had told him. Men were gathered in groups in the roadway and on the post veranda, and now Cap hurried his pace.

It took him only seconds after stopping at the first group to learn what had happened. Trooper Ryan's severed arm, a silver dollar in the palm, had been found on the post veranda by Calhoun when he went to open the saloon. It was plainly a warning to the town, everyone agreed, and Cap felt a momentary chill of fear. Maybe this was the beginning of what they had dreaded for so long. But the men in this group and in other groups were divided on what should be done. Most of them thought that, rather than wait for an Apache attack they should attack themselves and once more put the fear of the white man into the Apaches. They could send a messenger to Silver City and raise enough riders to raid the reservation and with a vengeance.

This sort of talk made Cap uneasy and he moved toward

the saloon door. It suddenly occurred to him that he was once and forever done out of Ryan's room and board bill and the thought made him irritable as he idly sauntered into the saloon.

The bar, Cap saw, was doing a booming business and he knew there'd be little work done today. The men who were drinking were even more vociferous about avenging Ryan. They were even arguing about who should lead the raid. The Army was being cursed for coddling the Apaches and for being scattered to all points of the compass when it was needed here. Calhoun, Cap noted sourly, was vastly busy pouring drinks and collecting money and he was paying no attention to the war talk. It gave Cap a small pleasure when he realized that Calhoun was working on an empty stomach.

At the far end of the bar Weymarn stood with his arms folded, leaning against the back bar. There was a scowl on his heavy face, Cap noted, and he guessed what Weymarn was thinking. Almost every man in the room, save himself, either worked on Weymarn's ranch or at his corral and stables, or freighted for him or broke his horses for sale. They were not at work and probably wouldn't be. This, too, gave Cap pleasure. He noted that Wilkie Brown was bellied up to the bar talking as vehemently as the rest of the customers.

Remembering Wilkie's visit of last night, Cap privately conceded that in the light of what had happened to Ryan, Wilkie was entitled to be afraid. Still, that didn't explain Wilkie's secrecy and his refusal to talk.

Cap would have liked to join the drinkers, but he knew he couldn't. He had neither money nor credit and as he looked at Weymarn he thought sourly, *An Apache's good for credit with him, but I'm not.* He felt a sudden rush of hatred for Weymarn and he wished there were some way he could hurt him.

On impulse then Cap moved on down the bar and halted before Weymarn who majestically turned his head, scowled at Cap and then looked back at his drinking workmen, many of whom were on their way to getting drunk.

"What you got your riders up to, Will?" Cap asked slyly.

Weymarn looked at him and the contempt he felt for Cap showed in his eyes.

"A dozen things usually, but not this morning," Weymarn said drily.

"I was talking to one of 'em last night," Cap said. "Scaredest man I ever saw."

"Anybody with any sense is scared nowadays. Maybe if Ryan had been scared he'd be alive."

Cap nodded sagely. "That's a fact," he agreed easily, and then he persisted. "This rider was specially scared, though, and plenty close-mouthed about what he was doing."

Weymarn looked at him steadily, and now Cap's glance slid away.

"Anyone who works for me better be close-mouthed or he won't work for me long," Weymarn said flatly. "My business isn't for barroom talk."

"Oh, I'm not curious," Cap said. "You got your hand in a lot of things that are no concern of mine."

"Right." Weymarn's voice was crisp.

"Still, you'd be a little curious if a man said he'd get shot if he told you what he was doing."

Weymarn's eyes looked suddenly sleepy and bored. "Somebody's been having fun with you, Cap."

"I know a scared man when I see him," Cap protested. "Besides he'd been paid good for this job because he was throwing money around like he was drunk."

"Did he say what the job was?" Weymarn asked coldly.

"Of course not, or I'd know," Cap said irritably.

Weymarn shrugged, and with indifference in his voice said, "I'm trying to run cattle and keep freight moving and I've got to do it even if some Apaches are loose. It's a risk my men take and I pay them well for it, Cap. If a man's scared, he can always quit."

Now Weymarn looked up the bar, a scowl coming onto

his face and then, as if he had come to a decision, he pushed away from the back bar and headed for Calhoun. Halting beside his bartender, Weymarn in a voice that reached every man in the room said, "Calhoun, close up! Get this crowd out and lock the doors. Don't sell any bottles."

"For the rest of the day?" Calhoun asked quietly.

"We'll see who's sobered up after supper." To the customers Weymarn said roughly, "Now clear out and get to work!" He paused. "If any of you have the sense the Lord gave you, you'll drop this talk about raiding the Apaches. Now get to work, all of you."

Grumbling their protests, the men at the bar and tables moved toward the door, Cap among them. Calhoun waited patiently until they were all out and then locked the big double doors. Hobbling back behind the bar, he ignored Weymarn as he surveyed the litter of glasses, bottles and cigar ashes on the bar. For the moment he was beat and he leaned against the back bar, feeling his good leg trembling with weariness, reminded by his hunger that he had barely eaten last night and not at all today. Moving his head, he saw Weymarn stuffing a handful of cigars into his vest pocket.

"We might as well call this a holiday all around," Weymarn said resignedly. "I'm going out to the ranch." He looked over at Calhoun. "Use your judgment about opening up tonight. If they drink too much, close them out again."

Calhoun only nodded and now Weymarn tramped up to him. "Belle told me what happened yesterday with that stage fare."

Calhoun shrugged. "He'd probably been tipping the bottle all morning."

"She shouldn't have been in here in the first place," Weymarn said, and then asked bluntly, "Why was she?"

Calhoun thought quickly. "I think she was worried whether I could manage bartending with this leg. As a matter-of-fact I wasn't doing so well. I was sitting down to rest at one of the tables when she came in. The drunk off the stage mistook her for a house girl. I hit him when he tried to make her have a drink with him."

Weymarn dipped his big head in acknowledgment. "That won't happen again. I'm obliged to you."

Turning, he walked out of the saloon into the store, and now Calhoun looked again at the mess on the bar and the floor that was littered with cigar butts. He had a sudden, almost overwhelming urge to clear out of this smoky, liquor-smelling room, into the sunlight and open country. *In a few days,* he told himself grimly.

For the second time that day he swept out the saloon and while he worked he was remembering Weymarn's words. Apparently Weymarn had accepted his harmless lie about Belle's reason for being in the bar, because Calhoun knew that if Weymarn suspected he and Belle had known each other, he would have, in his blunt fashion, voiced his suspicions. If Calhoun had confirmed them, he supposed Weymarn would have told him immediately to get on his way.

Now his thoughts turned toward the strange events of the morning and he began again to speculate on Ryan's death. If there was any connection between Ryan and Weymarn, there must be a clue to it somewhere. Mutilation was no new thing with the Apaches, but the fact that they wanted to call it to Weymarn's attention nagged at Calhoun's curiosity.

Finished with his sweeping, he came to his decision. His questions must be guarded so as not to arouse curiosity, and he would start with Hallie. Letting himself out the front door and locking it behind him, he swung down off the veranda and headed toward the Thompson cabin. Almost all of the men he had moved out of the saloon were in the road or on the veranda where they were still arguing about retaliation. One of the men called to him as he passed, "Want to go Apache hunting, Calhoun?"

Calhoun shook his head. "I don't." He passed them without stopping and the old anger stirred within him. There would be the loud-mouths among them who favored a raid, but, lacking whisky, they would become much less vocal as the day wore on. There would be others, and he hoped they would be the majority, who would point out that Ryan was nothing to them and ask why they should risk their necks for an anonymous white soldier. Calhoun was reasonably sure that the men who wanted a raid were too few in number to attempt it and that they would wait for reinforcements. That would take time and time would cool their anger.

Cap had come and gone with the news of the discovery of Ryan's arm. Hallie and Sam Avery, both a little sickened by the story, had returned to their work in the wash house. Sam was cranking the wringer handle as Hallie deftly fed the rinsed clothes into the wringer. Hallie's apron over her short-sleeved dress was made of oilcloth to protect her against the sloshed water and it gave her the appearance of a small girl who was playing at keeping house with the first thing that had come to hand.

She dipped her hand into the cloudy water and felt around the bottom of the tub and said, "All done, Sam."

"I'll help you hang them," Sam said.

"You don't need to. That's the easiest part."

Sam only smiled, picked up the basket and stepped out into the bright sunlight where the clothesline stretched from the wash house to the cabin. Silently then she began to hang up the clothes and Hallie's thoughts turned again to her father's news. Did this mean that any man caught alone by the Apaches could expect torture, death and mutilation? It had been bad enough before when, hanging up her washing, she had imagined the willows and cottonwoods on the stream bank as peopled with hiding Apaches. Now it could be true. She looked over at Sam now and was deeply thankful for his presence.

A movement at the corner of the house caught her eye and she saw Calhoun round the corner of the cabin, his

crutch gritting rhythmically on the gravel of the path. She
dropped the shirt she had just picked up and wiping her
hands on her apron, moved toward him. Approaching, she
noted the weariness in his long face and saw perspiration
beading his mustache. She knew it still hurt him to walk and
that he would never admit it. He smiled as she came up to
him and then his glance lifted beyond her and he said,
"Hello, Sam."

"Dad told me you were the one who found—it, Keefe."

Calhoun only nodded and the expression in his dark eyes
was sober.

"It's dreadful!" Hallie said vehemently. "They're ani-
mals!"

"But they always have a reason," Calhoun said mildly.

"What reason this time?" Hallie's tone was bitter.

"I don't know, Hallie."

Now she remembered and said, "You haven't had any
breakfast, have you, Keefe?" Sam came up then and Hallie
continued, "Let me put the rinse water on the stove and I'll
get you something."

"That's not in the bargain," Calhoun said firmly. "If I
miss breakfast, I miss it. And pay for it."

"I'll get it for him," Sam said.

"All right, Sam. Coffee's on the back of the stove and the
pancakes are in the warming oven." She looked at Calhoun.
"At least you'll eat that little, won't you?"

Calhoun smiled. "If Sam will bring me a cup of coffee and
hand deliver the pancakes without a plate, I'll sit on the
chopping block and watch you work."

Sam nodded and went on into the cabin while Calhoun
moved over to the chopping block and lowered himself onto
it. He took off his hat then, wiped his brow with his sleeve,
and then laid his hat on the ground. *He's doing too much,*
Hallie thought with concern, and she was about to return to
her clothes when Calhoun said, "Hallie."

She glanced at him and then moved over to stand in front
of him.

"You didn't tell me about you and Sam," Calhoun said.

Hallie felt her face flush and oddly she felt a faint irritation. "There's nothing much to tell."

"But you're engaged."

Was she, Hallie wondered? How long had it been since Sam had asked her? Two years. How long had it been since he'd even mentioned it? Months and months. It was as if he had regretted ever asking her and, she thought with honesty, it was as if she had been trying to forget it too. "Kind of," she said in a small voice.

"Well, that means marriage, doesn't it?"

She supposed it did—some day. But that day was far away. She refused even to think about it, and she said almost brusquely, "That's a long way off." She was suddenly both angry at herself and embarrassed. She wanted desperately not to talk about this. For something to say to change the subject she said, "Will there be a burial service for Ryan?"

"Someone will find the body and then there will be, I suppose," Calhoun said. Then he asked idly, "Did you see Ryan after his fight with me?"

"I looked in on him before I went to bed. Why?"

"Did I tear his uniform?"

Hallie tried to remember. Ryan had been sleeping on his face when she had looked in on him. "I don't think so," she said slowly. "I didn't notice it. Does it matter?"

"Just curious," Calhoun said.

Sam came around the house then holding a cup of steaming coffee in one hand and the pancakes in the other. He gave them to Calhoun who began to eat and now Hallie returned to the clothes basket. Calhoun's questions about her marriage still disturbed her and now she looked at Sam, trying to see him with the eyes of a stranger. He was an ordinary looking man, maybe shorter than average, but then she was too. He was friendly and helpful, but at the age of thirty-five he was still working for other men and was content to do so. He was quiet to taciturnity and he could talk

about few things but horses. He had almost no earthly pos-
sessions and no ambition to possess any. He didn't drink or
smoke and he accepted his modest lot with a lack of protest
that sometimes angered her. Yet she liked him and was used
to him and she suddenly wished that their relations would
never change from what they were this moment.

Sam came over now to help her and presently Calhoun
rose.

"You're a very good cook, Sam," Calhoun called.

Sam looked over at him. "Oh, I never cooked those. I can
make good ones, but Hallie made those."

Hallie looked over at him. "Oh, Sam, he's teasing you!"
she said almost sharply.

Sam gave her a slow smile as Calhoun said, "I'll try yours
some other time." He turned and hobbled up the path and
was lost behind the corner of the house.

"I guess I don't catch on very quick," Sam said mildly.
Hallie was sorry she had spoken so sharply. But Sam's
words to Calhoun had been so typical in their lack of humor
or of understanding of the character of the person who was
talking to him. He was so good, Hallie thought—and so
dull.

As Calhoun rounded the house he was weighing the information Hallie had given him. Ryan had been in uniform at
nine o'clock on the evening of his disappearance. If he had
changed out of it after that, where did he get the clothes to
change into and why did he want to change? Calhoun wondered. When he reached the alley that ran alongside the post
he saw the crowd had thinned considerably; he turned down
the alley toward the stables, swung past the loading platform, crossed the stable lot and came up to the big corral.

A stablehand was finishing harnessing a team to a buckboard just outside the corral gate, and now Calhoun leaned
against the corral and watched him, listening to the pleasant
racket coming from the blacksmith shop next to the stable.

The stablehand was dirtier than necessary, a young man

who liked to talk to horses and whistle as he went about his chores. When he had finished and wound the reins around the seat spring, he ambled over to Calhoun.

"Some business this morning," he began.

"Not so good," Calhoun agreed.

"A man shouldn't travel alone nowadays. That's what I told the boss a while ago when he told me to hitch the team. I said to him, 'Going alone's bad enough, but a buckboard can't lose anything except another buckboard if you're chased.' "

Calhoun nodded agreement to this sage observation and looked over the horses in the corral. He exclaimed softly, "Well I'll be damned." He turned to the stablehand. "Isn't that a Cavalry horse?"

"Sure, that trooper's that was killed."

"The Army didn't take this horse with them, then?"

"No. Left him here along with yours."

"Well, what did Ryan ride then?"

"Can't figure it out myself," the stablehand said.

"Did he steal one of yours?"

"That's just it." His speech was thoughtful, deliberate. "You never know around here. Some mornings I get up and find a couple of new horses in the corral. Other mornings there'll be two, three gone. The hands from the ranch come in at all hours and if their horses are fined down they'll swap."

Calhoun said idly, "Then Ryan could have taken a horse and nobody'd know it."

"Give the boss a little time and he'd know it, but I don't figure I would."

Pushing away from the poles, Calhoun said, "When I want to steal a horse, I'll remember that."

The stablehand was laughing uproariously as Calhoun wearily turned and headed for the stable and his cot in the stall. If it was possible for Ryan to take a horse and not have its absence remarked, then this could have been where he got his mount, Calhoun thought.

He turned into the stall, which was in semidarkness, and tiredly slacked onto the cot and lay down. *Damn this leg!* he said to himself in disgust. He was the next thing to helpless, and it seemed to him that the least movement took a monumental effort. Still, if memory could be trusted, each day it was getting less sore and took more of his weight without pain.

Closing his eyes, he tried to sort over what he had learned this morning since he had found Ryan's arm. It didn't add up to much. Starting out with his unprovable hunch that somehow Ryan and Weymarn were connected, he knew from Hallie that sometime in the night Ryan had traded his uniform for civilian clothes, and that he could have taken one of Weymarn's horses without its being missed. All this was in the pattern of the classic deserter, except for two related questions left unanswered: How did Ryan get civilian clothes and why was the severed arm left at Weymarn's? There was another question, perhaps unrelated to any of this. Why had Weymarn suddenly been so insistent that Bates get the shovel, which would have steered him away from the storeroom, and why had he proceeded quickly himself to get the tarp he had just ordered Bates to fetch?

So I can't find answers and if I could they shouldn't matter to me, he thought. He was eating and earning money to pay for his food; he slept under shelter; his leg was healing and he'd soon be able to ride out of here. He cared nothing about anybody he'd met here—with perhaps the exception of Hallie. He was sorry for her and would have liked to help her if it had been in his power. Then stay out of it, reason said.

But he knew he wouldn't. There was a white man dead and mutilated, part of his body defiantly tossed on the veranda of a country store. Given enough whisky, enough time for courage and anger to return, enough time for the word to spread and reinforcements to be recruited, this community of frightened men would turn on the Apaches and raid them—any Apaches. Years ago a mob of white men, angered by the killing of a prospector by a bad Apache, had ridden up from Tucson to Camp Grant and had massacred an innocent band of Apaches—men, women and children—who had been assured the protection of the Army.

Now, if the men of Weymarn's Crossing rode out, and if there were killings—and there couldn't help but be—it would further inflame the younger Apaches and so anger the older ones that they would join with the young bucks in a massive retaliatory raid. It had happened before, and always through stupidity on both sides. If Ryan's death could be explained and reasonable men on both sides could mete out a just punishment, maybe a cruel, savage and endless warfare could be averted. If not, then this time they had Maco to lead them.

So now he put his thoughts again to one of the unanswerable questions—the storeroom that Weymarn was so anxious Bates should not go into. Noon hour was approaching. Weymarn was apparently ready to drive out to the ranch, since the team and buckboard were waiting. Mrs. Weymarn would have to eat, leaving a lone clerk in the store. He could simply walk into the storeroom on the pretext he was looking for saloon supplies.

He sat up now, leaning his back against the wall, afraid that if he lay down he would go to sleep and miss Weymarn's departure. It was only a matter of minutes before he heard Weymarn's deep voice questioning the stablehand, followed by the sound of the team and buckboard in movement.

In another few minutes the racket at the blacksmith shop ceased and Calhoun knew the noon hour was here. He gave himself another ten minutes, then rose and hobbled out into the sunlight, turning toward the post. Laboriously, he climbed the steps to the loading platform, entered the store, walked past the door to the storeroom and Weymarn's desk and then looked down the store. The lone man clerk looked up from waiting on a customer, recognized Calhoun, nodded and Calhoun walked into the saloon. Putting his hat on the bar, he waited a moment, then hobbled back into the store and, without looking behind him, headed for the store-room, opened the door and went in, softly closing the door behind him.

The room was large, filled with barrels and crates at the far end stacked almost ceiling-high. There were shelves holding canned goods along one wall and on the near wall to the left there was a row of nails from which hung worn coats, a vest, a bridle and a pair of boots with the laces tied together. Evidently, Weymarn used this as a handy place to change clothes, Calhoun thought.

But now he was in here, what was he looking for? It was something that Weymarn had suddenly remembered he didn't want Bates to see.

Moving into the room, he looked about him and now he felt both angry and foolish. What did he expect to find, and how did he know what Weymarn didn't want Bates to see? Maybe he was looking at it right now.

Stubbornly, he moved on toward the corner where the coil of new rope Weymarn mentioned stood upended. The tarp had been on top of that, according to Weymarn.

Calhoun stood against it and looked around him. To his left was a stack of crates piled haphazardly. Ahead of him there was nothing but a nail in the wall. He was about to turn around when his glance fell to a strap that poked out from behind the lowest crate. Curious, Calhoun reached down to pick it up. It seemed to be firmly anchored and he tugged at it.

Slowly he pulled at the strap and saw that it was a belt. As he drew it up, a pair of pants attached to it followed.

Then Calhoun saw the yellow stripe down the outseams, and knew they were cavalryman's trousers.

Reaching far in behind the crate he drew out a Cavalry blouse and crushed trooper's hat.

Looking down at them, Calhoun thought grimly, *Ryan's, of course.*

"Looking for something, Mr. Calhoun?"

Calhoun wheeled, the clothes in hand, and saw Belle

Weymarn standing in the doorway. They looked at each other a long moment in silence, and Calhoun knew a swift and sudden bitterness. He'd been caught and she would tell her husband and Weymarn would kick him out. *Or will she tell?* Calhoun suddenly wondered. *Or maybe she already knows about the uniform?* It was useless to lie about what he was looking for; it was in his hand.

"I was," he said slowly. "I found it."

Belle Weymarn came slowly across the room and looked down at the uniform, then looked at Calhoun, her expression one of puzzlement.

He might as well tell her all of it, he thought bitterly.

"Ryan's," he said quietly.

She hesitated, then asked curiously, "Why does that interest you?"

"Did you know it was here?"

"No." She paused. "Does it mean something?"

"Only that Ryan was on an errand your husband knew about when he was killed."

Belle Weymarn's green eyes widened. "How do you know that?"

"Ryan wasn't in uniform when he was killed. This is it. Where did Ryan get clothes to wear if not from your husband? What's his uniform doing here?"

"But we sell clothes to anyone. They can change in here."

"On credit? Ryan was broke. In the middle of the night, too?"

Belle Weymarn was frowning and her glance never left Calhoun's still face. "What are you trying to tell me?"

Calhoun sighed. "I don't know myself. All I know is that this morning your husband denied Ryan was working for him. I know he sent a man in to get a tarp that was on this coil of rope, then remembered the uniform and got the tarp himself. I think he hid Ryan's uniform at the same time."

Belle Weymarn still looked puzzled and now a little wary. "What does this all prove?"

"That your husband knows why Ryan was killed. That

Ryan's arm the Apaches left here this morning was some kind of message to your husband."

"And why does it interest you?" Belle asked again, almost angrily.

"Doesn't it interest you?" Calhoun's voice was quietly savage. "It better. A white man has been killed and mutilated. The men outside are already talking about getting even. If they try, that means dead Apaches—just any Apaches, not the ones who killed Ryan. And that means the Indians will get even. They'll wipe this town out like so much smoke. They'll know who to hit too. They'll hit your husband and everything he owns." He paused. "You."

Anger had drained from Belle Weymarn's eyes and her face had gone pale. "What are you going to do?"

"I know one thing I'm not going to do. I'm not going to ask your husband why Ryan was killed."

Belle hesitated. "No."

"I know something you're not going to do, too. You're not going to ask him." He paused to lend emphasis to what he was about to say. "If you did, I think you'd wind up back in the Happy Days. What do you think?"

"I think I would, too," Belle Weymarn said bitterly.

After supper Calhoun returned to the post and saw that only a handful of townsmen were loafing there in the hopes that the saloon would be open.

Hobbling down the veranda he said as he passed them, "Let's go easy on the booze and heavy on the cards tonight."

Unlocking the door in the dusk, he entered the dark room, pulled down from their hangers the two overhead lamps and lighted them, tied on his apron and took up his position behind the bar.

The games of cards were started and as if by common consent the talk veered away from Ryan.

Calhoun served a couple of bar customers; then, moving away from them, he leaned against the back bar and folded his arms. He was wondering again as he had wondered all afternoon if he could trust Belle Weymarn to keep silent. She knew only as much as he did, that her husband was up to something that had caused Ryan's murder. Plain fear should keep her silent. If it didn't he'd know shortly, for if she talked then Weymarn would ask him to move on.

A player left the table, came up to the bar and asked for some cigars. Calhoun extended the box, the player helped himself and Calhoun tossed his money into the cash drawer before he again leaned against the back bar. All he knew for certain now was that Ryan had been on an errand for Weymarn that had so angered the Apaches that Ryan had been killed and his arm defiantly returned to Weymarn. But what Apaches had Ryan seen and on what errand? Only Weymarn himself knew that, Calhoun thought bitterly.

Cap Thompson wandered in then with his pinochle cronie, old Bailey Harris, and for a while the two of them watched the poker players and talked with them idly. At the conclusion of one conversation Cap looked up suddenly and eyed Calhoun. Presently Cap moved over to the bar in front of Calhoun and rested his elbows on it. This posture shoved his high shoulders higher, making him look almost deformed. His petulant face seemed so pale and soft in the lamplight that it looked almost boneless and his eyes held an open malice.

"Hear you're out of a job," Cap said.

"It's news to me, but I'm glad to hear it," Calhoun said idly.

"Gus Henry got back tonight." Cap paused. "What about the board bill you're owing me?"

"It's owed Hallie," Calhoun corrected him. "She'll get it when I'm paid. Now go back to your card game, Cap."

Reluctantly Cap turned and he was halfway across the room when a deep voice boomed from the veranda door, "Give me a hand out here, four of you."

Calhoun turned his head to see Weymarn hulking hugely in the doorway, the black night beyond him. He was dressed in clean range clothes and halfboots and wore a buttonless vest over his shirt. Before anyone could respond to his request, he said, "Calhoun, there's a lantern under there at the head of the bar. Light it and bring it out."

Now the closest players at the first table rose, looked at one another and headed toward the door as Calhoun moved up, found the lantern, lighted it and went out onto the veranda.

The sudden light from the lantern revealed Weymarn's team and buckboard. In the bed there was a mound of something under a canvas tarp.

Weymarn stepped heavily off the veranda, went up to the buckboard and yanked off the tarp.

Calhoun raised the lantern for more light and then he saw a man's body, eyes open and unseeing, one hand close to his head, lying on the buckboard bed. His whole shirt front was stained with long-dried blood.

"Wilkie Brown!" someone exclaimed from behind Calhoun. Then recognition came to Calhoun. This was the puncher who had shared his stall last night. Now his glance lifted to Weymarn who, with both hands on the side of the buckboard bed, was looking soberly at the dead man.

Weymarn's big head lifted and he regarded the man on the veranda. "I found him just off the road on the way to the ranch," he said calmly. "It's plain ambush. His rifle was in its scabbard, his gun in its holster."

"Apaches?" someone asked.

Weymarn's big shoulders lifted in a shrug. "I'm not sure, but I wouldn't think so. Because whoever got him rode a shod horse." Now he pushed away from the buckboard. "Me, I'm going to have a drink."

By now the saloon was empty, and the card players stepped down into the road to get a closer look. Weymarn hoisted himself to the veranda and saw Cap standing back against the wall, a look of distaste on his face.

Weymarn took Cap's arm, saying quietly, "You look like you need a drink, too, Cap."

Together they went into the empty saloon and parted, Weymarn going behind the bar, Cap going up to it.

Weymarn reached for a bottle and two shot glasses and poured out two drinks, then he looked squarely at Cap and said in a soft, serious voice, "It was Wilkie Brown you said was so scared, wasn't it, Cap?"

Cap nodded. "I never said, but it was."

"Look what happened to him," Weymarn said.

"I said he had something to be scared about. You didn't think so."

"You don't see it."

"See what?" Cap added irritably.

Now Weymarn drank his shot, then wiped his mustaches with the back of his hand. He had never ceased looking at Cap. "I think Wilkie talked too much, maybe to you, Cap." He paused, watching the beginning of a startled expression come into Cap's face. Then he went on, "You might know what got Wilkie killed and not know you know it."

Again he paused. "If I were you, I'd forget everything that Wilkie told you, Cap. I'd never talk to anyone else about it—or they might be after you, too."

Cap's face drained of color and he looked at Weymarn, finally comprehending this raw, flat and unmistakable warning.

Suddenly his eyes seemed to roll up in his head, and he fainted.

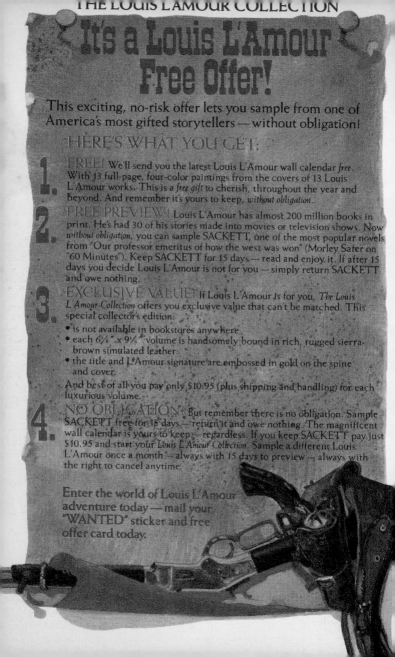

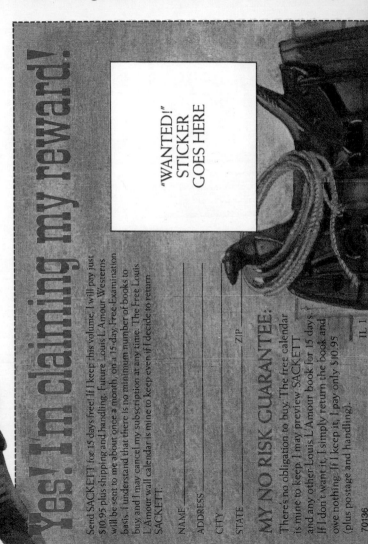

Track down and capture exciting western adventure from one of America's foremost novelists!

• It's free! • No obligation! • Exclusive value!

4

Next morning Calhoun came to work as usual. He found the saloon doors open and a bald, heavy-set man in shirt sleeves was sweeping the floor. Calhoun halted in the doorway to rest a moment and now the man came up. "You must be the Calhoun they told me about."

Calhoun dipped his head in acknowledgment. "You're Gus Henry. I guess I'm out of a job."

"Looks that way."

"I'm not sorry you're back."

"I am," the bartender said grimly. "I don't like what's going on around here. First that trooper and now Wilkie Brown." He hesitated. "You think it was the Apaches that got Wilkie?"

Calhoun knew he must answer with care, since the bartender was the fount of all information to the townspeople. He said, "It's not likely. At least Weymarn didn't think so. Has Weymarn come down from upstairs?"

"He's at his desk," Henry said. "Anything I ought to know?"

Calhoun smiled. "Nothing I can tell you." He hobbled on past the bar and now, on this even floor, he tested his leg, putting more weight on it than he ever had before. It could almost take his full weight this morning. Perhaps if he kept off it today he could discard his crutch tomorrow.

Moving through the connecting door into the post, he saw Weymarn seated at the desk beside the crude railing. When he hauled up beside Weymarn, the older man looked up, smiled and said, "Morning, morning."

Calhoun bid him good morning and then observed, "I see Gus is back."

"That's right." Weymarn smoothed down his big mustaches with his huge palm and exhaled deeply. "Things were coming so fast last night, I plain forgot to tell you he'd be back." As if this reminded him of something, he frowned, asking, "How's Cap?"

"All I know is that he didn't show up for breakfast this morning."

Weymarn nodded thoughtfully. "Some people can't look at a dead man," he growled. "I think I'm one of them."

Calhoun asked curiously, "You have any notion who killed Wilkie?"

Weymarn eyed him steadily. "A very good one."

Calhoun waited.

"The Apaches killed him," Weymarn said.

"That's not what you said last night."

"Of course I didn't," Weymarn smiled faintly. "If I'd told the truth last night we'd have a saloon full of men getting liquored up right now, ready to ride out and murder some 'Paches. This time they'd do it, not just talk about it like they did when we found Ryan's arm." He paused. "I can tell you the truth because I don't think you're one of these 'Pache-hating hotheads. I'd appreciate your keeping it quiet and I think you can see why."

Calhoun nodded, but he thought immediately *Why is he telling me?*

Weymarn went on, "I'm sure it was 'Paches because Wilkie's horses were gone. There were two sets of moccasin tracks and two sets of hoofprints, both unshod."

"That adds up," Calhoun conceded.

"It scares a man," Weymarn said thoughtfully. "If I'd left an hour earlier, it could have been me."

"That's a fact," Calhoun said idly. Then he shifted his crutch. "Mr. Weymarn, I owe a board bill with the Thompsons and I've got no money."

"I'd forgotten." Weymarn rose, went over to the safe,

reached in the cash drawer, counted out an eagle and five silver dollars, returned to the rail and handed them to Calhoun. "That ought to hold you until you can straddle a horse again."

"That'll be soon. Thanks."

Calhoun turned away and walked up the aisle. Belle Weymarn was standing beside a crate from which she was transferring clothing to one of the middle tables. Halting beside her, Calhoun touched his hat and said, "I'd like a couple of pigs of lead and a pound of black powder, Mrs. Weymarn."

"Maybe we all should buy the same," she said tonelessly.

While she went back to the powder shed, Calhoun hobbled behind the hardware counter and hunted till he found the slabs of lead under the counter. He was remembering Weymarn's words of only a minute ago and again he asked himself, *Why did he tell me?* Before talking with Weymarn, he had been only mildly curious as to who killed Wilkie and why. He would have accepted Weymarn's story without question, but now Weymarn had told another story, plausible enough, and asked him to believe it. Why? Now he saw Mrs. Weymarn approaching and he came to his decision. He would go see for himself which story was true.

Belle Weymarn set the whisky bottle holding the powder on the counter alongside the two pigs of lead, and said, "Anything else?"

Calhoun shook his head and laid his money on the counter.

"It seems Ryan wasn't the only one the Apaches didn't like," Belle said quietly, watching his face.

"So your husband says."

"You think Wilkie Brown was on some secret errand for Will when he was killed?" she jibed.

Calhoun felt his face flush. "That never occurred to me."

"It will," Belle said coldly. She picked up the money, went behind the counter to the cash drawer and laid his change on the counter. Calhoun picked up his change, put a pig of lead in each hip pocket, took the bottle of powder in his free hand, touched the brim of his hat and went out.

As he hobbled down the street toward the Thompsons', he thought of what he must do. If he went to the corral, saddled his horse and rode out, the word was sure to get back to Weymarn, whose suspicion might be aroused. There was a way around that, he thought, and he turned in the Thompson gate.

This was Hallie's day to bake, Calhoun remembered, since he had seen the big pans of dough atop the stove at breakfast time. First knocking on the doorframe, he stepped into the kitchen which held the good yeasty smell of baking bread. Hallie had cleared the big table and on its floured oilcloth she was kneading the dough, dividing it and placing it in a half dozen pans to rise.

Turning at Calhoun's entrance, she smiled over her shoulder and Calhoun, taking off his hat, limped across the room, pulled a chair out from the table, placed it against the wall, put the lead and the powder on the floor by the chair and sat down. Hallie, he noticed, seemed happy, perhaps because this was bake day and not another wash day. Her black hair was held back by a gay red ribbon.

"Did you have to close again?" Hallie asked.

"No. Gus Henry's back and I'm out of a job."

"Are they guessing who killed Wilkie?"

"Not that I've heard."

Hallie worked in silence a moment and then asked, "What will you do with all your time now?"

"I guess I'll spend the money Weymarn gave me." He added idly, "What kind of a place has he got?"

"The ranch? Oh, it's not much to look at, but he runs a lot of cattle out there. Sam would know."

"Where is Sam?"

"He's cleaning out the wash house this morning."

This was luck, Calhoun thought, and he asked, "Just where is the ranch?"

"Eight or ten miles south of here."

"How do you get there?"

Hallie ceased work and thought a moment. "Cross the creek and take the first left-hand road." She went on telling him which roads to ignore and which to take. Calhoun wasn't listening. The buckboard tracks would tell him. Instead, he was wondering how Hallie would accept what he was about to say next.

When she had finished speaking, Calhoun said, "I think I'll ride out that way and have a look."

Hallie looked startled. "You won't, Keefe!"

"Why not?"

"You aren't able to ride!"

"How do you think I got here?" Calhoun asked drily.

"But you can't even walk yet!" Hallie protested vehemently. "I won't let you!"

"You're kind of little to stop me," Calhoun said, and smiled.

Hallie came around the table now and stood before him, her eyes bright with anger. She put her flour-covered hands on her hips and said flatly, "You've got to have a horse. If you start out of this door, I'll beat you to the corral and turn your horse out. And I'll tell Weymarn not to let you have one of his."

Calhoun sighed softly. He knew Hallie would do just what she said, and that would kill any hope of leaving without arousing Weymarn's suspicions. He came to a decision then he knew he might regret, but he had no choice now.

"Hallie, listen to me a minute."

"I'll listen to you an hour, but it won't change my mind!" Hallie said flatly.

"I want to find out how Wilkie Brown was killed."

Hallie frowned. "Why, he was shot, wasn't he?"

Calhoun nodded. "Weymarn told everybody last night that Wilkie Brown was probably ambushed by a white man, since he saw tracks of a shod horse. But he told me this morning with nobody around to hear him that the Apaches killed Wilkie. He said he told his first story because he didn't want to rouse the town again so they'd move against the Apaches." He paused. "Which story is true?"

Hallie thought a moment. "Maybe his story to you. I can see that the men here might be mad enough to go after the Apaches if they thought Indians killed him."

"Why did Weymarn tell only me and ask me to keep it quiet?"

Hallie looked at him steadily, her eyes troubled. "I don't know."

"I know, Hallie." Calhoun brought the edge of his palm down on his knee with a cutting gesture of emphasis. "I think he's afraid I'll be curious about Wilkie Brown's murderer if I believe Wilkie was killed by a white man. Weymarn thinks if I believe Wilkie was killed by Indians, I won't be curious at all."

Hallie was silent a minute. "But why should you be curious if a white man killed Wilkie?"

Should he tell her of Wilkie's drunken disclosure about Maco which he didn't know if he really believed himself? No, this was not the time. Instead, he said, "I think Wilkie Brown knew more about Weymarn's business than he should have."

"What do you mean, Weymarn's business?"

"Do you think Weymarn is honest?"

Hallie frowned. "I always thought so."

"I know he sells whisky to the Indians. I saw him deliver two gallons to an Indian wagon." Hallie's lips parted in surprise and Calhoun went on, "All this is why I have to ride out today without Weymarn knowing it. I'm not going to the ranch. I'm going to find out if Wilkie was killed by Apaches or by a white man."

"How can you tell?"

"I'm a fair country tracker," Calhoun said drily. "It's the way I make my living." He paused. "Now will you let me ride out?"

Hallie turned away from him and slowly walked back to the table. "What do you think Weymarn is up to?"

"I can't tell you yet. I don't know if he's up to anything. It's just that I know Weymarn is a liar, I know he sells whisky illegally and I think he might be in something worse than that. I want to know what it is."

"What if he finds out you're suspicious?"

"He won't unless you tell him, and I don't think you will." Calhoun smiled and Hallie, watching him, smiled shyly in return.

Now she lifted a chunk of dough and held it in her hand, her eyes musing. "How will you get your horse without Weymarn knowing it?"

"That's where Sam comes in, Hallie. He can go over to the corral, pick up my saddle in the stable and tell the hostler I've asked him to exercise my horse since I can't ride myself. He can ride it into the brush across the creek where I'll be waiting."

"Will you tell Sam the real reason you want it?"

"I don't think he'll ask," Calhoun said drily.

Instantly Hallie looked at him and he held her glance. He hadn't meant his irony to be so plain, but now that she understood him, he asked, "Will he?"

"I guess not," Hallie said softly.

Now Calhoun rose. "I don't know when I'll be back, Hallie. It may be late."

"Will you be careful, Keefe?"

"As careful as I can. And that's mighty careful."

He smiled at her as he went out and he knew that her glance followed him as he stepped out the door and turned toward the shed.

Inside the wash house Sam Avery was working at wetting down the rammed earth floor and tamping it with a log to which was nailed a heavy piece of board. At Calhoun's entrance Avery looked up, his face dripping with perspiration.

"That's work," Calhoun observed. "I think you need a break from it, Sam."

"Oh, this is too heavy for a one-legged man," Sam said and his slow smile came.

"No, I wasn't figuring on spelling you. I was just wondering if you'd do me a favor."

"Sure."

"You figure you could go over to the stable, get my saddle in the stall where the cot is and tell the hostler I asked you to exercise my horse since I can't ride him?"

"You want me to exercise him?"

"No. Just ride him across the creek into the brush. I'll be waiting there."

Sam looked puzzled. "You mean you're going to ride him?"

Calhoun nodded. He looked out toward the cabin as if to make sure no one was around and then said quietly to Sam, "I don't want Hallie to know. She'd raise Cain and threaten to put me to bed. You know how women are."

Sam smiled. "I know, but still your leg isn't so good."

"It's plenty good," Calhoun contradicted. "Riding is easier than walking, and you know it. If you can help me in the saddle I'll be all right. Now go ahead, Sam. Not a word to Hallie."

Avery looked dubious, but he managed a smile. He went out now and cut behind the empty cabin next door on his way to the corral. Calhoun went out, turned to his left and hobbled the thirty yards to the stream. Without halting, he waded across it and the cold water that seeped into his boots held a welcome coolness.

In a few minutes he heard a horse splashing across the ford and then Sam, mounted on the gelding, pulled in behind the screen of willows.

Sam dismounted and Calhoun, rubbing his chestnut's muzzle, took the reins. Now Calhoun handed Avery his crutch, saying, "Stand that up in the brush when I'm gone, will you? No. Better do it now so I can see where you put it."

Standing on one leg, Calhoun watched him hide the crutch.

"Now come over and let me put my arm around your shoulder, Sam."

Avery came up and Calhoun, grasping the saddle horn with his left hand, put his arm around Avery's shoulder. Now, leaning his full weight on Sam, he lifted his left foot into the stirrup.

"Now heave and straighten me out, Sam."

Avery lifted his weight until Calhoun could take it with his left leg. Now he stood in the stirrup. The bite would come when he swung his injured leg over the saddle. Lying flat on the chestnut's neck, he slowly lifted his leg and the bite did come. Gently then, he lowered his right leg and straightened up, putting his full weight into the saddle. There was an ache, but no real pain, and now he looked down at Sam.

"Thanks, Sam. And not a word to Hallie." He rode off without looking behind him.

As soon as the road climbed out of the creek bottom it forked, and immediately Calhoun picked up the two sets of tracks left by the team and buckboard. They were the freshest tracks and, at first, as he rode along the bench heading south, he paid no attention at all to them. The road was little more than a track through the scattered piñon and cedar, and now Calhoun checked his impatience. For more than an hour he rode steadily as the road climbed into the foothills of flinty rock and gravel. To the west he could see the far reaches of the timbered mountains, while this was an empty and desolate country which bordered on being desert. The two sets of buckboard tracks of Weymarn's coming and going were occasionally lost to him on rocky ground, but he rode ahead with the confidence that he would pick them up later, which he did.

Presently he was in canyon country and the road climbed steadily until it broke through the rimrock onto a mesa thickly studded with piñon that somehow had succeeded in finding root and growing into this sheer rock wasteland. Here Calhoun halted and for many minutes watched his back trail; he saw no movement of any kind and, when he was satisfied that he was not being followed, he continued on.

He soon slowed his pace then, scanning the flat stretches of rock for the occasional telltale streaks of white rock dust left by the tire irons of the jolting buckboard and the shod team.

He had traveled more than two miles from the rimrock when his horse suddenly pricked up his ears and snorted uneasily.

Calhoun reined up and looked about him. Ahead of him was a thick clump of piñons through which the road seemed to go. Touching his chestnut's flanks with his heels he rode on, but now his horse seemed reluctant to head for the piñons and seemed to want to skirt them. Firmly then, Calhoun held him to the road and he had ridden thirty feet when he saw a stain under one of the piñons. Approaching, his chestnut danced uneasily, and then Calhoun reined up beside the stain and looked down.

This, he knew, was where Wilkie Brown's body had been and the stains were dried blood. Now he saw the faint marks of the buckboard tire irons. Riding beyond the piñons, he picked up old tracks, but there was no indication that the buckboard had been driven past the stain.

In the dirt-filled crevice he saw the marks of the boot heel in the sandy soil and he thought, *Probably Weymarn's.* Remembering Weymarn's story that there were moccasin tracks and the tracks of unshod horses, Calhoun began his circle of the area, the first a tight one around the clump of piñons. The rocky ground told him nothing, and now he widened his circle, searching for patches of earth that would yield a print.

His second circle also revealed nothing and now Calhoun reined in and looked to the west where the mesa joined the climbing foothills, perhaps a half mile away. If he could get off this caprock, his chore would be much easier, and now he turned his chestnut toward the west.

As he had guessed, the caprock gave way to gravel and dirt where the foothills lifted above the mesa. Now Calhoun turned south and rode to the far edge of the mesa before putting his horse up the slope of the foothills. Then, turning north, he slowly traveled the side of the foothills, his glance on the ground alongside him. Once he reined up to study the ground and moved on past what he recognized as old deer tracks.

He had gone perhaps a quarter of a mile when he came upon the fresh tracks of two shod horses on the gravelly steep hillside. The horses had slipped and braced themselves for the descent, leaving long furrows in the gravel. Calhoun put his horse up the hillside, paralleling his tracks and presently achieved the crest. Here, gravel gave way to dirt and Calhoun had his look. These were shod horses and they were headed east, in the direction of the road over which he had come.

Calhoun leaned far over in the saddle, studying the imprints, memorizing their size and the characteristics: one of the horses wore shoes which were light ones and worn on the outside at the frog.

All this told him was that a pair of riders had recently come from the direction of the mountains. He moved on now, keeping the same course across the face of the foothills, and presently he saw that he was nearing the north edge of the mesa. He had only a hundred yards to go to the edge when he reined in abruptly, then turned his chestnut up the slope. There, alongside him, were many tracks on a faint trail. As he had done before, he climbed his horse paralleling the tracks until he achieved the crest of the hill where the gravel gave way to eroded dirt. There were, he saw, three sets of tracks, all made by shod horses, and heading toward the mountain. The most recent tracks were made by one of the same horses that had made the first set of tracks. Three men, then, had ridden toward the mountains, two had returned.

Curious now, Calhoun followed the tracks as the game

trail wound through climbing foothills that still held only cedar and piñon. He could see now that the trail was dipping down into a steep timbered canyon, and then he observed that one set of tracks veered off while the other two clung to the trail. It took him only a moment to learn that it was the last rider who left the trail. It was this rider who interested Calhoun most; since he had followed the other two and returned. Now Calhoun pushed on, following the single set of tracks. It took him along the canyon edge, over ground that climbed steadily. Calhoun followed for an hour along the canyon rim before the tracks suddenly cut off the rim and angled along the canyonside to the bottom of the canyon. Here a small seep, a third of the way up the slope, nourished a tangle of willows and alders before its water vanished into the thirsty canyon bottom. The rider had let his horse drink and then had tied him in a willow thicket. Circling the seep, Calhoun picked up the tracks of a man walking downcanyon and into the thicket.

Calhoun felt a sudden excitement now as he put his chestnut into the thicket. Breaking through the other side, he reined in instantly. On the rocky ground beyond the thicket he saw a saddle lying on the ground alongside a loaded pack frame. Slowly riding up, Calhoun saw a rope and a bridle thrown on the ground.

He turned downcanyon then, picking up the tracks, and twenty yards away saw the marks where a horse had reared and pitched. Only a few feet down the canyon was a dark spot crawling with ants and flies. This, then, was where something had been killed.

Now Calhoun tried to add this up. A single rider had followed the two horses, a saddle horse and a pack horse. He had circled them and lay in wait to ambush the rider leading a pack horse. After making his kill, he had freed the two horses. The man killed, Calhoun knew, was Wilkie Brown.

Now Calhoun tried to sort out the story in the confused tangle of tracks. Returning to the pack frame, he saw boot

tracks and horse tracks heading in the direction of where the
body had lain and he supposed that the killer had unloaded
the pack horse, led it to the body and loaded the body upon
him. Dropping downcanyon, Calhoun tried to pick up the
tracks of the killer and the pack horse heading back toward
the road, but they were not there.

Returning, he circled the saddle and pack frame, heading
upcanyon, and immediately picked up the tracks of the two
horses, the one that had been tied at the seep and presumably the pack horse. He followed this set of tracks to the
canyon rim and then reined in. He was certain that if he ran
these tracks out, they would turn out to be the first pair he
had encountered—the pair headed toward the road. The
killer then had ambushed Wilkie Brown in the canyon and
had deposited him in the piñons alongside the road where he
would be discovered by the first passer-by.

Now Calhoun looked at the sun. It was heeling over behind the mountains, and Calhoun knew that he would have
to work fast between now and sunset to learn the one thing
he needed to know: Where did the killer come from?

Now he put his horse in motion along the rim heading
east and soon picked up the three sets of tracks. When he
came to the spot where he had first cut the tracks, he continued backtracking until he was on the rocky mesa bed. The
going was slow now and he could see the scuff marks on the
rock of shod horses. Presently he came to the road where it
broke through the rim and now he reined up. The scuff
marks indicated that some horses had come through the
break and immediately turned west. Had the killer ridden
out with Wilkie, pretended to part with him, circled and
ambushed him? Calhoun didn't think so because when two
riders leading one pack horse rode together, the pack horse
was usually last. This time the rider was last, which indicated that he had followed later.

If the killer had been waiting here on the rim, chances
were he would have hidden himself somewhere in the opposite direction from which Wilkie Brown would turn. And

now Calhoun put his horse in motion, crossed the road and moved between the clustered piñons. Immediately he reined up and saw the scuff marks left by the buckboard tires. For a puzzled moment he wondered what the buckboard had been doing off the road, and then he moved on. Twenty yards farther he had his answer.

Reining in, he read the story. Close to one of the piñons there was dung and signs of stalling which argued that a horse had been tied to the tree for some time. Calhoun was sure of this when he saw the many marks of the buckboard tire irons and the scuffed rock where only one horse had stomped the ground in impatient waiting.

Only one horse, he thought. And then it came to him with a calm certainty. Weymarn, driving the buckboard, had come up the road through the break in the rim, pulled off the road, cut out one of the horses in the buckboard team, tied the remaining horse still hitched to the buckboard to a tree and had ridden the cut-out horse after Wilkie Brown. He had circled Wilkie, shot him, loaded his body on the pack horse and had dumped it farther on up the road. Then he had returned to the buckboard, hitched up his saddle horse and had driven on to where Wilkie's body lay under the piñon. To anyone but the most careful observer, it would seem as if Weymarn, on his way to the ranch, had discovered Wilkie's body. All the tracks indicated this. The rocky ground would give few clues to the curious and certainly no man would contend that a buckboard was a vehicle a killer would use to overtake and track down a victim.

Wearily, Calhoun carefully withdrew his feet from the stirrups and let his legs dangle, resting the hurt one. Folding his arms he leaned on the horn, pushed back his hat and looked again at the tire-scuffed rock. *If Weymarn killed him, what was it for?*

What if, Calhoun theorized, his hunch about Wilkie having seen Maco was right? Wilkie worked for Weymarn, so he would have told him. Maco was shot in the leg, Wilkie had said, so he would have had a hard time traveling. *What if he isn't traveling?* Calhoun thought suddenly. *What if he's holed up hiding and that was where Wilkie saw him?* But Weymarn would know that, since Wilkie worked for him. Suddenly, Calhoun remembered the pack load of grub. *Going to Maco?* But it didn't make sense for Weymarn to hide and feed Maco who was every white man's enemy.

Suddenly, the thought came to him *Hiding him, hell; he could be holding him.* Not for the Army, Calhoun thought, or he'd have got word to Fort Kelso by the first stage. *Then for what?* Maco was of value only to the Army. *Only?* No, he was also of value to a bunch of savage Apaches who needed him for a leader. Was Weymarn holding him in exchange for something the Apaches could give him?

On the heel of that question he had asked himself, Calhoun thought of Ryan, and a sudden excitement came to him. Ryan could have been Weymarn's messenger to the Apaches! He, an unknown man to the Indians, could never be traced back to Weymarn; he could have carried Weymarn's proposition. If that proposition had been unsatisfactory to the Apaches, Ryan would have started back to Weymarn with the news. The Apaches, following him and seeing his destination, could have killed him, butchered him and defiantly deposited his arm on the porch of Weymarn's store.

If Calhoun's theorizing was right and Weymarn had Maco, then the reason for Weymarn's killing of Wilkie Brown was clear. Weymarn was running the risk of Federal imprisonment for hiding Maco. Drunk, Wilkie Brown was a talker. If he said enough to Calhoun to make him suspicious, couldn't he have said more to other people? Weymarn couldn't afford to let him live; he had to silence him.

Now Calhoun straightened up, only now noticing that dusk had come. *You don't know a damned thing for sure,* he thought disgustedly. *All this is guessing.*

Now he kneed his horse around, returned to the break in the rimrock and put his horse down the road in the lowering dusk. Now he had a theory—and it was only a theory, he thought—he could move. First, he had to find out if Weymarn really held Maco. The place to find that out was on the reservation, not by searching a whole range of mountains. Who had Ryan delivered Weymarn's message to? It couldn't have been to anyone else but Santiago, Maco's young lieutenant on his last break from the reservation, his good friend and his blood relative. Santiago was as mean and vicious as Maco, but he lacked Maco's brains and endurance. Santiago was perfectly capable of butchering Ryan as he would butcher a steer. No, he wouldn't go to Santiago because there were other ways, Calhoun thought grimly.

Before he reached the creek in the darkness, he came to his decision. Tomorrow he would go to the reservation and get the proof he needed.

In the willows beside the creek he found his crutch that Sam had stood on end so that he would not have to dismount. He took it across the creek and rode in behind the Thompson cabin where a light was still burning. It took him three tries before he could get his leg over the saddle and by that time Sam Avery had come out of the kitchen, rifle in hand.

"It's me, Sam," Calhoun said. "Can you sneak this horse back? Throw the saddle in the wash house."

"Sure," Sam said. He came out, took the reins from Calhoun and said softly, "Hallie's on to you."

Calhoun watched him go off in the darkness, leading his horse, and then he turned to the kitchen door. Hallie was framed in it, and as he came forward she said, "Oh, Keefe, thank the Lord! I was afraid you'd been bucked off."

"No, riding's easier than walking, Hallie," he said as he hobbled in and took off his hat.

"Did you find out what you wanted?" Hallie asked.

Wearily Calhoun settled himself in a chair, leaned his crutch against the wall and looked soberly at Hallie. "I found out. Weymarn killed him."

For a stunned instant Hallie regarded him with only shock in her eyes. "Weymarn! You're sure?"

Calhoun nodded. "He was driving a buckboard and heading for the ranch. He knew Wilkie was heading into the mountains with a pack horse. Weymarn pulled off the road, cut out a horse from his team, followed Wilkie, circled him and ambushed him. He brought the body back to the road to make it look as if Wilkie had been killed there." He paused. "Then he rode back to the buckboard, put his horse back into the team and drove along the road to discover Wilkie."

Hallie was silent a long moment, watching him closely. "But why, Keefe, why?" she asked then.

Calhoun shook his head. "I don't really know, Hallie. I've got a notion, but I can't prove it—not until tomorrow anyway."

"What happens tomorrow?"

"I'm going to the reservation."

Hallie took a step closer to him and said softly, vehemently, "Ride on through the reservation, Keefe! Keep going, stay out of here!"

Calhoun frowned. "Why?"

"You're in danger!" Hallie said passionately. "I didn't know it until you told me this."

"I don't see that." Calhoun was puzzled.

Hallie hesitated. Then said quietly, "Weymarn came here today looking for you."

Calhoun felt a faint chill touch his spine. "What did you tell him?"

Hallie shook her head, as if to rid herself of the memory. "It wasn't much good, Keefe, but I think it might have worked. Dad was in the bedroom with the door closed. When Weymarn knocked and stepped through the door and asked for you, I had to think fast. I put a finger to my lips, pointed to the bedroom and whispered, 'He's asleep'."

"Did he believe you?"

Hallie nodded. "I think so. He said he'd see you later." She paused. "Keefe, don't you see what that means?"

Calhoun nodded. "He's suspicious, but I think you threw him off, Hallie."

Hallie shook her head violently. "What if he finds out that you know all about him?"

"Remember, I'm supposed to be crippled and not able to ride. It's natural enough I'd sleep on my first day off and I couldn't sleep in the stable on account of everybody working." He smiled. "Everything hangs together, Hallie. He won't find out."

Hallie said soberly, "I still wish you'd ride through."

Calhoun said teasingly, "Your Dad wouldn't let me. He'd miss my board money."

"You can't pay your board bill if you're dead!" Hallie said vehemently.

Calhoun heard footsteps outside and shook his head in warning. Then Sam Avery stepped through the door and he was grinning at Calhoun. "Well, Hallie found out about you anyway, Calhoun."

"I guess I rode just a little too long," Calhoun said easily.

Breakfast next morning was a strange affair. Cap Thompson, looking sick and unaccountably wearing shell belt and gun, was silent to taciturnity. Hallie, in the presence of her father and Avery, could not take up her arguments of last night and Calhoun knew there was much she wanted to say. Last night, interrupted by Sam, he had had no time to explain to her his plan. If this time Weymarn inquired for him, she would have to plead total ignorance of his whereabouts.

As he rose from the table and headed for the door, he caught Hallie's eye and winked. He saw her shy answering smile begin and he knew she meant to wish him luck and to warn him to be careful.

Outside in the warm sunlight he found himself thinking of Hallie, and of Sam too. The ways of women were unaccountable, he reflected. Sam, with little laughter in him and less ambition would make Hallie a sorry husband. She would still be young when he was middle-aged. Some men,

Calhoun thought, were born to a life of puttering. They helped wash dishes, cut wood, carried water, set tables, started fires and fed dogs, but they never left their mark on a country or on a job of real work. Sam was one of these men and Hallie knew it, yet she would marry him. Calhoun felt sorry for her and obscurely angry with her at the same time.

On the way to the road now, Calhoun lifted his crutch off the ground and tested his leg. This morning it held his weight and he knew he had no real need for the hoe handle. However, it was needed to impress Weymarn with his inability to move around. Hobbling up the street, he climbed the post veranda and went into the store and unnecessarily bought a bandanna handkerchief from the male clerk. Mrs. Weymarn was not around, but Weymarn was seated at his desk in the rear. Calhoun made a point of waving at him and Weymarn lifted his big hand in reply and returned to his book work. Since Weymarn obviously had nothing to say to him Calhoun turned and went out.

Once on the street Calhoun turned right toward the four corners and hobbled leisurely across them, taking his time and enjoying the morning. At his first pause to rest himself he glanced back at the post. Weymarn was nowhere in sight, and Calhoun was certain then that he was no longer curious. He limped past the last couple of houses and then continued along the rutted stage road until the Crossing was hidden from sight by a wind-blown sandy ridge. Now he tossed his hoe handle away and seated himself in the shade of a piñon. Presently he heard the stage approaching and rose. The teams came over the ridge, then the stage appeared, and now Calhoun raised a hand. The driver recognized him, pulled in his teams and braked the coach to a halt.

"Got room for one more, Hobie?" Calhoun called.

"All the room there is. I ain't got a fare." He was a bearded, taciturn man past middle age, who opened his mouth only to relay the necessary gossip demanded of all stage drivers.

Gingerly, favoring his leg, Calhoun climbed up into the box beside him and Hobie cursed his teams into motion.

"Kelso for you?" Hobie asked.

"No, the agency."

The driver sank into silence and Calhoun was grateful for it. He wondered now which one of the many Indians he knew on the reservation he could go to. Most of his friends were of the older generation of Apaches who had long since seen the futility of violence. They were not likely to know any of the plans or hopes of the younger rebels. Calhoun knew some of these, too, but he also knew some of the younger men who were violently opposed to Maco's and Santiago's ambitions. It was to this group he must go for information and he finally decided Mahtla was his man.

It was early afternoon when they came to the forks where the road to the agency turned west and the Fort Kelso road continued straight ahead. Far down the Kelso road a banner of dust rose and trailed and Hobie, as he pulled his teams left on the agency road, observed, "Troopers movin' this way."

"Hear of any trouble?"

"Fellow killed south of the Crossing couple of days ago, but they tell it wasn't 'Paches."

Calhoun said nothing as he watched the dust banner until it was hidden beyond a rise of land. The first scattered earth and grass wickiups of the Apaches now began to appear and in front of each were naked brown children who waved to Hobie and were ignored by him. As they rolled into the agency where a few scattered cottonwoods gave some shade Calhoun saw that the U-shaped adobe agency building facing the distant mountains had been completed since his last visit. The stage pulled up before the big log building of the agency trader; Calhoun and Hobie swung down and Calhoun paid his fare.

A dozen Apache ponies lined the tie rail and in the shade of the veranda a handful of Apaches squatted against the wall out of the sun. They were all dressed more or less alike in breechclout, long leggings rolled down below the knee, and tattered shirts worn tail out. Some wore uncreased Stetsons and those who did not held their long black hair away from their faces with a headband of red flannel. The women were formless in their blankets.

Inside the post, which held much the same goods as Weymarn's, Calhoun bought some shag tobacco and cigarette papers and stepped out into the sun. The Apache police building across the way had four ponies at its tie rail, and Calhoun knew that already his presence would have been noted by them and that he would be unobtrusively watched.

He struck west now, afoot, past the wickiups of the Indians who chose to live close to the post. Presently, he came to an irrigation ditch with planted fields beyond, and now pausing occasionally to rest his leg, he followed the ditch toward a low hill against which he could see the cluster of wickiups he remembered so well. These were the wickiups of the Coyotero tribe families whom he had helped move to the reservation five years ago. As an agency packer he had helped move five hundred of them four hundred miles to their new home within the agency, and during the weeks on the trail he had learned to admire and respect these people. Betrayed by a succession of treaties, starved and swindled by military and civilian agents, they had nevertheless obeyed the summons to settle near the agency, where they had been peaceful and law-abiding.

The dogs picked him up when he was not far from the wickiups and to their chorus of barking he entered the village. Women were working hides beside their wickiups and now Calhoun saw an old man sitting in the shade of the frame where one of the hides was stretched. It was Tana, old when Calhoun last saw him, and now Calhoun went up and spoke to him. The old man remembered him and now Calhoun, who knew the language, passed out the shag tobacco. Other men and women and children, of course, gathered around in friendly and curious fashion to observe this tall white man who dwarfed them. Calhoun greeted those he remembered, asking about families, numbers of children and the state of the crops. Most of the younger men, he learned, were working on the new irrigation ditch for wages of fifty cents a day.

After a while he moved on, not seeming to be in any hurry, but only interested in how his old friends were doing. He was almost through the village when he saw Alope, Mahtla's wife, standing before her wickiup, smiling shyly. He was speaking to her, asking the same questions about the family, when he felt a touch on his elbow.

Turning, he saw Mahtla, who was smiling in greeting. Calhoun put out his hand and the two shook hands warmly. Mahtla was tall for an Apache, younger than Calhoun, and he had a broad sunlined Apache face and aquiline nose. On the long trek to the reservation they had become fast friends and each time Calhoun passed this way he visited Mahtla and his family. He had taught Calhoun more of the Apache language than Calhoun had been able to teach him of the English, and now, after inquiring of his family, Calhoun asked in Apache, "Still trading horses, Mahtla?"

"To blind men," Mahtla said, and smiled.

"You don't own a horse I couldn't beat riding a goat."

"If you bet your goat I'll race you."

Alope laughed and Calhoun said easily, "Let's see what I have to beat."

Mahtla pointed with his chin to the brush corral at the far end of the village; Calhoun said good-by to the girl, and together, he and Mahtla walked up to the corral. He wanted this visit to look natural, as if he were visiting all his old friends, and he knew the girl would repeat his joking with Mahtla.

Once at the corral, which held almost a dozen horses, Mahtla pulled some brush aside and Calhoun entered. Now Calhoun said quietly, "Point out your horses Mahtla, but let me talk. I need your help."

Mahtla lifted his hand, as if pointing to a horse. "I hear you."

"Do you know where Maco is?" Calhoun looked at him now.

Mahtla's dark glance held his, and then slid away. "You don't know what you are asking."

"I do know. You'd be killed if anyone knew you talked."

Mahtla moved off and around a horse, so that he could see the village, and Calhoun followed.

"Is this for the agent? The police? The soldiers?"

Calhoun shook his head. "For me only."

Mahtla looked at him steadily. "I have heard, friend, but I have shut my ears." He hesitated. "Why do you want to know?"

"I want him back in jail," Calhoun replied evenly. "If he's loose, you know what it will bring down on your people?"

Mahtla nodded once. "I know." Then he said quietly, "A white man holds him."

"Weymarn?"

"Yes."

"Where?"

"Santiago's band, the Chiricahuas, don't know. They are looking for him."

Calhoun felt a growing excitement, and now he asked, "What does Weymarn want with him?"

"I have only heard it whispered and I shut my ears. He wanted fifty horses and a hundred cows." He paused. "Santiago's band could not pay."

Now he had it all, Calhoun thought.

5

When Will Weymarn acknowledged Calhoun's greeting that morning he had half a notion to call him back, engage him in conversation and try to learn exactly what Calhoun had done yesterday. Then he decided against it, wondering why he was concerned about it at all. There was a reason, though, for his concern and he knew what it was; he had told Calhoun an unnecessary lie yesterday about the Apaches killing Wilkie, and Weymarn was realistic enough to know that it was the unnecessary lies that trapped a man.

He watched Calhoun hobble out, his limp still pronounced, and the sight of the crutch gave Weymarn a faint reassurance. The man couldn't even walk yet, let alone ride.

He heard someone approaching from the rear door and looked up as Belle halted by his desk. She, too, was looking at Calhoun, and now her glance dropped to Weymarn. "It doesn't look as if he'll be riding for some time," she observed. Then she asked, "Are you going to give him work, Will?"

"I thought I might put him at the mill when this scare blows over. Just because we can't haul everything we cut, Kennedy is dogging it. We ought to have cut lumber stacked a mile high."

"What are you waiting for? He can walk."

"For his leg to heal. Kennedy'll fight him and he better be in shape."

Belle smiled faintly, nodded, slipped her canvas apron over her head and went up front to take her place at the counter.

Weymarn watched her go, admiring her fine figure, and he returned to work. Unknowingly Belle had reassured him about Calhoun. The man couldn't ride, and even if he could, what would prompt him to check on Wilkie Brown's death? Only one thing, Weymarn reflected; Calhoun ate with the Thompsons and Cap, not intentionally but inadvertently, might have dropped something that made Calhoun suspicious. *You're making up trouble when you've got enough already,* Weymarn thought derisively.

Now he rose, suddenly too restless for work, and moved out through the rear door onto the loading platform. He shoved his big hand inside his shirt and scratched his chest, and now he felt the old gloom, mingled with exasperation, return. What was he going to do with Maco? He couldn't deny that he was no nearer a deal with Santiago than when he'd sent Ryan over. There must be some way, somehow that he could use him.

The trouble was, this bunch of wild, young Apaches had no money and no goods. There was no reward out for Maco's capture either. Climbing down the steps, Weymarn suddenly knew the depths of total frustration. He held something immensely valuable to a people who had nothing of value to exchange for it, and every day he held Maco the danger increased.

He remembered now, tasting the irony of it, how elated he had been the night Maco announced himself. That night Weymarn had closed the store and, in darkness, left the veranda, rounded the corner of the post and had his foot on the first step of the outside stairs that ascended to his living quarters upstairs.

A voice whispered from under the stairs, *"Nantan!"*

Only one person had ever called him Chief, and that derisively.

"Quien es?" he had asked in Spanish, but he already knew who this Chiricahua was.

"Maco."

He had stepped down and gone behind the stairs. Risking

a light he struck a match and saw Maco, small, wizened, his eyes glittering like a snake's, crouched there. He wore only headband, breechclout and leggings, and on his right thigh were great gobs of mud around which blood was oozing.

"I am hurt, Nantan. Hide me until I am well."

Maco had every right to claim help, Weymarn knew; they both were so deeply involved in past unlawful business together that each could hang the other. Weymarn had supplied Maco with guns and ammunition which Maco paid for by appropriating to himself his tribe's government issue beef and fighting anyone who protested. But always they had been equals, made so by their strength; now Maco was helpless.

It had been simple enough to reassure Maco, go back to the stable and rouse Wilkie Brown and Ollie Matson. He wouldn't have chosen them above all his other hands for this mission, but they were the only men available. They were to take Maco outside the settlement to a place Weymarn designated, tie him up and guard him until Weymarn came out in the morning. The three of them had gone back to Maco and it was Weymarn who laid his gun alongside Maco's head and knocked him unconscious.

The following day Weymarn, Maco and his two guards rode up to the Blue Bell Mine, deep in the mountains. The ladder in the shallow shaft was loosened, Maco forced to descend and the ladder withdrawn. Maco was his prisoner.

But what for? Weymarn asked himself now. Descending the steps he rammed both hands in his hip pockets and strolled over to the corral, folded his arms and looked over the horses. He saw Ryan's horse there and supposed he'd have to return him to the Army when they next came through. Off by himself was the big chestnut of Calhoun's, and Weymarn admired him.

Weymarn heard someone approaching and slowly turned his head to see Sam Avery, a bundle of dirty clothes under his arm, ready to cut across the stable lot on his way to the Thompsons'. When Avery saw Weymarn, he came over to him, halted, and asked in a respectful tone, "We going to haul this week, Mr. Weymarn?"

"Later on," Weymarn said. Suddenly he remembered that, after noting Calhoun's horse was gone yesterday and remarking it to the hostler, the lad had said Avery had been sent by Calhoun to exercise his horse. Now the faint uneasiness over Calhoun's whereabouts yesterday returned to him and he said idly, "That's a nice-looking horse of Calhoun's. Did you really run him yesterday?"

Avery grinned and shook his head. "I only rode him across the creek."

Weymarn scowled. "You didn't bring him back till after supper."

"I didn't have him. Calhoun had him." Again Sam grinned. "He didn't want Hallie to know he was planning to ride with that hurt leg. She'd of stopped him for sure. So he had me get his horse and meet him beyond the creek."

Weymarn felt cold fear touch his spine. "You mean Calhoun can ride?"

"Good as ever."

"Where'd he go?"

"He was heading south the last I saw." Now Sam turned and said, "You want I should get in touch with you later in the week?"

Weymarn only nodded, his thoughts in a turmoil. Calhoun was able to ride and he had ridden south, presumably to check on Weymarn's story that Wilkie had been killed by the Apaches. Weymarn was certain of this. If Calhoun hadn't wanted to deceive him, he would have come and got his own horse instead of sending Avery. Moreover he had even lied to Avery about his reason for sending him. But what really clinched Weymarn's belief was that Hallie Thompson had lied about Calhoun being asleep in the next room when Weymarn had returned from Wilkie's funeral. She was covering for Calhoun while he snooped.

Calhoun had been gone yesterday from morning until after dark, plenty of time to travel to the seep and read the story and return. Straightening up now, Weymarn knew that Calhoun's actions had changed from the possibly suspicious to a real threat, and he must be taken care of. Turning now, he walked past the corral and stables, moved around a freight wagon minus a wheel that was up on blocks and halted in the big doorway of the blacksmith's shop. Tom Jeffers, the blacksmith, was heating the tire preliminary to putting it on the wheel that leaned against the anvil. His helper, a gangling boy of fourteen, was operating the bellows.

When Weymarn walked in Jeffers looked up. "Can you spare Earl for the rest of the day, Tom?"

"As soon as we get this tire on."

Weymarn nodded and looked at the boy. "Ride out to the ranch, Earl, and tell Wes Bolton to come in."

The boy nodded, and now Weymarn turned and went out. Yes, this was for Bolton, Weymarn thought. He could not only do it, but he would like doing it.

Now Weymarn's thoughts returned to Calhoun. Calhoun could suspect anything he wished as to who killed Wilkie Brown, but he would have a hard time proving anything, Weymarn thought, as he recalled the terrain in which he had chosen to stage his discovery of Wilkie Brown's body. A bloodhound would have a hard time tracking a horse across that rocky mesa top.

What, Weymarn asked himself, was Calhoun's next logical move? He might suspect Weymarn, but he had no hint that Wilkie had been killed to stop his chatter about Maco. As long as Calhoun was ignorant of Maco's imprisonment he had nothing to fear immediately from him. All Calhoun could really prove was that the Apaches had not killed Wilkie and that he, Weymarn, had lied.

Weymarn went on about his daily business now, and he was strangely untroubled. After dinner he sat on the veranda and smoked two cigars, hoping to catch sight of Calhoun. He did not see him, but he was really not worried.

Calhoun's horse was still in the corral and he was probably lazing around Thompsons'.

It was past mid-afternoon when Weymarn, working at his desk, heard the sound of many horses on the street outside. He rose, tramped the length of the store and joined Belle in the open doorway. There in the street were six mounted Cavalry troopers and a gray-haired lieutenant whom Weymarn knew. The lieutenant dismounted now, gave his reins to one of the troopers, and they moved on to the creek to water their horses. They looked at the saloon with obvious longing, but the lieutenant turned his back to them, pulled off his gauntlets and tramped up the steps.

"Hello, McKelway," Weymarn said. "Still chasing Indians?"

Lieutenant McKelway touched his hat brim to Mrs. Weymarn and said, "Not this trip. Right now I'm hunting whisky. Seen any?"

Weymarn smiled faintly. "I think I have." He stepped out onto the veranda and joined McKelway who was already on his way into the saloon.

Weymarn remembered when McKelway first came to Fort Kelso and even then he had been known as the oldest second lieutenant in grade in the Army. A more forceful man, seeing his ambition thwarted by lack of promotion, would have resigned his commission and long since have gone on to other things. McKelway, however, was not a man of ambition; he wanted only drink and lots of it and his food, shelter and clothes provided him. As a soldier, he did exactly what was asked of him and no more, and his round ruddy face held a strange, almost touching contentment.

There were two or three idlers in the saloon, among them Cap Thompson, standing at the bar and Weymarn noted with surprise that there was whisky in front of Cap. He looked weak and scared and his glance would not meet Weymarn's as he nodded to McKelway.

"Hello, Cap," McKelway said. Then he added, teasingly,

"As a military man, why aren't you out fighting the Apaches like the rest of us?"

Cap smiled weakly. "I'd like to be, that's for sure."

McKelway now observed the two shot glasses and the bottle that had been placed before him and Weymarn. He shoved his shot glass back and said, "Give me a water glass." He turned to Weymarn and said, "How are things here, Will?"

Weymarn lifted his heavy shoulders in a shrug. "Everybody seems to be waiting for the Apaches, but they don't come." He asked idly, "You after Maco, too?"

McKelway took two deep drinks from the water glass he'd half-filled with whisky. After asking for cigars, he turned to Weymarn and shook his head. "No, the major sent me to investigate Ryan's death." He took out a small notebook from his blouse pocket along with the stub of a pencil and he opened the notebook on the bar.

"The major wasn't in any hurry, was he?" Weymarn asked drily.

McKelway chuckled. "If he had been would it have changed anything?"

"I guess not," Weymarn said. "What is it you want to know?"

"Just what you can tell us."

Weymarn told him of Ryan's being ordered out of the saloon, of his drunken fight with Calhoun and of his disappearance. When he told of finding Ryan's severed arm, McKelway grimaced. He made no mention of Ryan's being out of uniform. Summing it up, Weymarn said, "I figure he was deserting and ran into a bunch of Apaches."

"Why leave his arm here?" McKelway asked.

"They probably knew he was in the detail that had attacked them. Maybe it was just their way of showing they'd got even. I don't know, really."

McKelway, who had been writing, nodded, closed his book, put it in his pocket and took another drink. Firing up a cigar, he asked, "Has the body turned up?"

Weymarn only shook his head.

"That'll be something for my men to think about on the ride to Silver City, just in case they're thinking of deserting."

"Hasn't the Army got better things to do than send you to Silver City, Mac?"

"This is no exercise. We're the paymaster's escort."

Weymarn's eyebrows lifted. "Only six men?"

"All we can spare, Will. G Troop and F Troop were sent north and I and part of F are chasing Maco. That leaves a few of us to housekeep and run errands." He grinned. "This is the kind of soldiering I like. The Huachuca escort hands the paymaster to us and we take him to Kelso. A four-day ride in the country with three-months' pay to wind it up."

Now he drank the remaining whisky, lifted a handful of cigars from the box, tucked them in his blouse pocket and said to Weymarn, "We'll be back through in three days, Will, and pick up Ryan's horse. See you then." He paid his score and walked out.

Weymarn walked with him to the veranda steps and watched him tramp out into the road where troopers, back from watering their horses, stolidly awaited him. He mounted, gave the order, "Forward by twos, march!" and rode off at the head of the column, turning south at the crossroads. He waved casually to Mrs. Weymarn as his detail pulled out.

Belle was standing with her arms folded, leaning against the doorframe, and now she asked, "Trouble somewhere?"

Weymarn shook his head. "He was checking on Ryan's death."

"Have you ever figured that out, Will?"

Weymarn looked at her for a still moment. "What's there to figure?"

"About the arm being left here."

"I think they were just spitting in the Army's eyes," Weymarn said easily.

Belle turned and went back into the store and Weymarn,

tramping down the aisle, had already forgotten the conversation with his wife. He was considering, with great care, the information McKelway had just given him.

Seating himself at his desk, he swiveled his chair so that he faced the rear of the building, put a big leg on the desk top and tilted his chair back. McKelway was headed for Silver City with a six-man detail to escort the paymaster from Silver City to Fort Kelso. The paymaster, Weymarn knew, would travel in a Douherty wagon whose teams would be driven by an enlisted man. The pay chest, double-locked, would be ironed to the wagon and would contain at least three-months' pay for every trooper, non-com and officer at Fort Kelso.

Only nine men counting McKelway and the paymaster, Weymarn thought, and he felt an increasing excitement. *There is Maco's ransom.*

For Santiago's band could wipe this detail out of existence. When they brought him the gold that was in the paymaster's chest, he would return Maco. Here was the solution to his troubles.

Carefully now Weymarn considered what he must do. Santiago, thanks to Ryan's bungling, already knew he held Maco, so it was senseless for him to act through an intermediary this time. He would see Santiago himself. Maco's Apache lieutenant would not harm him, he knew, for Maco's life depended on Weymarn remaining unharmed. The only thing that might make Santiago hesitate would be the fact that his attack would bring the Army down on him, but before the Army could act Santiago would have Maco and would be raiding and burning his way into Mexico.

All things considered, it seemed foolproof to Weymarn. Everything dovetailed so nicely that Weymarn thought he had earned himself a drink. He rose and went into the saloon.

The last customer had left the store and Weymarn followed her to the front door and locked it. He pulled down the first overhead lamp and blew it out and was reaching for the second lamp when he saw the tall, motionless figure leaning against the back door, thumbs hooked in his belt. Weymarn blew the second lamp, moving toward the rear of the store, and on his way he picked up the lamp off his desk and, carrying it, headed for the storeroom door.

"Come in here, Wes," he said.

Inside the storeroom, he set the lamp down on a crate and then turned to regard Wes Bolton, who had followed him.

"Shut the door," Weymarn said.

Bolton moved quickly, effortlessly; he closed the door and then he turned to regard Weymarn. His eyes were of a bleached-out gray set in a wedge-shaped, weather-blackened face that held a sleepy alertness. He was dressed in a puncher's working clothes and greasy Stetson, and save for a certain wariness in his eyes, he might have been any working rider. Weymarn knew he was not. Bolton had a talent for picking fights and winning them, so much so that he had left Silver City ahead of the sheriff. He was a bad drinker, mean and vicious, and Weymarn had learned to keep him far away from town, with its liquor and inevitable trouble.

Weymarn said, "There's a man hanging around here that I don't think you'll like."

Bolton considered this for a moment and then smiled faintly. "I don't reckon I will. Who is he?"

"Name's Calhoun. I don't think you know him."

Bolton shook his head. "What's he look like?"

"Oh, tall, wears a mustache, dark eyes, but none of that matters. You'll know him because he's limping around on a hoe handle that he's using for a crutch. Don't count on that crutch slowing him, though."

"Where do I find him?"

"He's sleeping out in the stables. That's where you'll sleep and you'd better make it happen right there, at night."

"Tonight?"

"Absolutely not," Weymarn said flatly. "I'm leaving here early in the morning and I want to be well out of the way when it happens." He paused. "Got a place you can sleep tonight?"

"I can find one."

"Then don't go near the stables. I don't want you to see him till I'm gone and I don't want it known that you've seen me tonight. Have you got that?"

Bolton nodded.

Weymarn said flatly, "Don't try to talk Gus Henry into selling you any whisky tomorrow, Wes. Gus's standing orders are not to serve you and when I get back I'll check to see if he did."

Bolton said nothing, only regarded him with chill eyes that revealed nothing of what he might be thinking.

"When I get back," Weymarn continued, "I'll give you a bottle for the trip back to the ranch. But no drinking here."

"What if I see him before tomorrow night?"

"Too risky. Tomorrow night there'll be no witnesses so it'll be easy to claim self-defense."

"This is for money," Bolton said quietly. "A hundred dollars."

Weymarn nodded. "I pay for what I get. Just deliver it first."

Next morning when the stage rolled to a halt in front of the agency traders, Calhoun saw that a passenger from Kelso had appropriated the seat by the driver: Calhoun climbed inside to take his place beside a woman and opposite two men who looked strangely uncomfortable in civilian clothes and who, Calhoun guessed, were troopers whose enlistments were newly up.

After the team change, the stage pulled out past the agency, and now Calhoun slumped down in his seat, pulled his hat down over his eyes and sought sleep. He was not in the mood for conversation. He had spent a sleepless night in the louse-infested blankets on the floor of the trader's second-story storeroom, and much of it had been spent in pondering his next move.

By daylight he had known what he was going to do. He reasoned that it would be senseless to go to the Army with the story that Weymarn was holding Maco. The moment Weymarn was confronted with the accusation, Weymarn could do one of three things: he could pass on the word to free Maco; he could order him killed; or he could laugh at the Army and dare them to show proof that he held Maco. Knowing the man as well as he did, Calhoun guessed Weymarn's choice would be the latter.

There remained then only one course for Calhoun. He must return to the Crossing, show Weymarn that he was able to ride, get a job working for him and find out where Weymarn was holding Maco. The only thing that really bothered Calhoun, however, was the possibility that Weymarn, unable to make a deal with Santiago and his Chiricahuas, might turn Maco loose. If he did that, Calhoun knew Maco would be off on a killing raid. But could Weymarn afford to turn Maco loose for fear of Maco's revenge? It seemed to Calhoun that Weymarn, like the man who mounted the tiger and could not dismount, had to keep Maco prisoner until some sort of exchange could be worked out.

Calhoun felt himself drifting off into sleep and gave himself to it. On the very edge of it he heard the stage braking to a halt, and now he opened his eyes and started to push himself erect when he heard the driver call out, "What are you doing in this patch of country, Will?"

"Got tired of counting money, so I thought I'd count a few Indians."

With immediate shock, Calhoun recognized Weymarn's voice, and now he sank slowly deeper in his seat. He knew from the direction in which Weymarn's voice had come that he was on the opposite side of the stage and a little ahead of it.

"Is Plummer at the store?" Weymarn asked.

"Was when I left."

"See any new lumber at his place?"

"Didn't look."

"Then I catch hell," Weymarn said easily. Apparently he saw the woman passenger for the first time and said, "Excuse me, ma'am."

Then the driver said, "See you, Will," and the stage creaked into motion.

When Weymarn was past, Calhoun shoved himself erect and pushed his hat to the back of his head. What was Weymarn doing on the reservation? The very fact that the driver had halted the stage and asked Weymarn that same question meant his visit was unusual. Calhoun didn't believe for a minute that Weymarn had ridden all this way to check on the delivery of the post traders lumber. A conference with Santiago? Calhoun doubted if Weymarn would do that until he remembered that Weymarn had power of life and death over Maco, and that Santiago, if he wanted Maco, could not afford to harm Weymarn. Had Santiago changed his mind and decided to deal with Weymarn? No, if that were so, Santiago would go to Weymarn, not summon Weymarn to him.

It could only mean, Calhoun decided, that Weymarn was resuming negotiations. This time did he have a different offer?

Belle Weymarn cooked an early breakfast for her husband, said good-by and afterwards opened up the store. Stepping inside, she welcomed the dim coolness, for the day was already warm and would be another hot one. Back in Weymarn's office space she opened the safe, took the change over to both cash drawers and by that time the first pair of customers came in. As she was waiting on them Gus Henry came in from the saloon, took down a can of tomatoes, got some crackers, put the money in the cash drawer and returned to the saloon. Without thinking about it, Belle supposed some rider, caught breakfastless, had sent Gus in to fetch him his morning meal.

Presently the other clerk came in and now Belle, with

some distasteful book work ahead of her, moved over to the doorway, put her shoulder against the frame and looked out into the street. Nothing ever changed here, she thought almost with resignation. There could be a man's arm left on the spot she was almost standing on; there could be a dead body brought in in a buckboard, but nothing really ever changed. The Campbell kids across the street would come in for their morning lollypops at the same time they'd come yesterday. There would always be three or four ponies standing hip-shot at the post tie rail. The same lackadaisical traffic of wagons and riders would continue tomorrow as it had continued yesterday. All this, half-pleasant, half-irritating dullness, was the security she had wanted, she thought, so she had no right to complain.

A movement at the far end of the veranda attracted her attention and she looked past the saloon doors and saw a man seated in one of the veranda barrel chairs. He had a can of tomatoes locked between his knees and, using his knife as a fork, was spearing the tomatoes and eating them. As he lifted a portion of a tomato up to his mouth and tilted his head back to catch the juice, Belle felt a sudden shock. This was Wes Bolton, she knew, and today Will, the only man who could handle him, was gone.

A sudden anger touched her. Bolton was forbidden to come to the Crossing except on specific errands, but here he was lounging in front of the saloon, probably preparing for a first drink. Maybe he'd had that already, Belle thought in exasperation, and she wondered what the day would bring if Bolton got drunk.

Stepping out onto the veranda, she walked toward him. Now Bolton, can in one hand, crackers in the other, came out of his chair. His pale eyes regarded her without interest.

Belle halted before him and asked coldly, "Does Will know you're here, Wes?"

"Sure, he sent for me."

"Sent for you?" Belle echoed, puzzlement in her voice.

"Didn't you meet him this morning on his way to the ranch?"

Bolton hesitated a moment and a look of uneasiness came into his face. Then he said, "Yes. He said for me to come here and wait for him."

"What for?"

"He didn't say," Bolton said levelly.

"Well, you'd better ride back to the ranch if you want to see him."

"No, ma'am, I don't think I'd better. I'll just wait."

"But he won't be home until tomorrow night," Belle said impatiently. "What do you propose to do for two days?"

"Wait."

"And drink?" Belle asked angrily.

"No, ma'am, just wait."

Belle hesitated. Had Will really sent for him? She wondered. Why would he if he were going out to the ranch today? She looked at Bolton, hating his stubbornness, but knowing that because she was a woman, even his boss' wife, he would not take orders from her. *Or will he?* she wondered.

She said now, "Wes, I don't think you're telling the truth. Now go back to the ranch where you belong and quit loafing around here."

"No, ma'am." Bolton's tone was both polite and adamant.

Belle, in anger and frustration, wheeled without a word and went back into the store. Twice that morning she looked out at the veranda and saw Bolton still seated in the end chair. She quietly checked with Gus to find out if Bolton had been served any drinks, and Gus stoutly maintained that Bolton hadn't even asked for one.

When she came back from her solitary noon meal, Bolton was still there and now Belle felt a renewed anger. Bolton hadn't come in to drink and apparently it hadn't occurred to him to visit with anybody while he waited for Will. He sim-

ply sat there like an Indian hour after hour, not even talking
with the other loafers on the veranda.

In mid-afternoon, Belle heard the southbound stage even
before it hit the four corners, and as she reached the door
and halted, the driver braked and brought the teams to a
halt with a flourish. The door opened and two men got out
and started for the saloon. Then Belle saw Calhoun step out,
speak to someone in the stage, touch his hat and turn toward the steps. Immediately, two questions formed in her
mind; she saw Calhoun look over the two or three idlers on
the porch, and then he saw her, and climbed the veranda
steps.

"Where's your crutch?" she asked.

Calhoun smiled faintly. "I never promised I'd keep it forever."

Belle smiled faintly. "Been traveling?"

Calhoun nodded. "To the agency." He paused. "I saw an
old friend of yours headed for the agency, too."

Belle said cautiously, "Did you?"

"Your husband."

Belle looked carefully at him and saw he was watching
her closely. She knew the denial was already in her face. "I
don't think you did," she said slowly. "He rode out to the
ranch this morning."

Calhoun suggested quietly, "Maybe he *said* he was going
to the ranch."

"Oh, no," Belle said. "See that man sitting in the end
chair? He met Will this morning on the way to the ranch."

Calhoun was silent a long moment. Then he said drily,
"All right. For some reason your husband doesn't want it
known that he was going to the reservation. So I didn't see
him. So it was somebody else."

Belle said, with swift impatience, "I don't know what
you're hinting at, but I don't like it!"

"I don't like being called a liar, either."

They looked at each other a long moment and then Belle
shook her head. "When he left, Will told me he was going to

the ranch. Wes Bolton saw him and he sent Wes into town to wait for him."

Without a word Calhoun turned and went into the bar-room and within seconds he came out with the stage driver. They halted in front of Belle and the driver touched his hat.

"Hello, Miz Weymarn."

"Tell her who you stopped and talked to this morning," Calhoun said.

"Why, it was Will. He was headin' for the agency for a powwow with Plummer over some lumber." The driver shook his head. "You shouldn't let him ride alone nowdays. Can't tell when some crazy Injun will jump him."

"I'll tell him," Belle said, and smiled, and the driver went down the steps to supervise the hitching of the fresh pair of teams that were being driven up.

Belle said quietly, "Will lied to me and Wes Bolton did too."

"Who's Bolton?"

Belle grimaced. "The toughest hand Will's got. Will keeps him out at the ranch because he's such a troublemaker Will doesn't dare let him come into town."

She saw Calhoun look carefully at Bolton who was still seated in his chair, and now a sudden bitterness was in her. Why was it necessary for Will to lie to her? Bolton must be in on it too, for he backed up Will's lie.

"Why do you think Will went to the agency, Keefe?"

Calhoun looked at her coldly. "Maybe he was hunting for the rest of Ryan."

Before she could answer, Calhoun wheeled and went down the steps, turning toward the Thompsons'. Weymarn, then, had lied to Belle about where he was going today and for some strange reason his man Bolton had done the same. He wondered now if Belle would tell Weymarn of her conversation with him, and he doubted it. If she hadn't told Weymarn of surprising him with Ryan's uniform, she wouldn't tell him this, and Calhoun hoped against hope that if Belle became suspicious enough of her husband, she could give him information that he had to have.

When Calhoun went through the Thompson gate, he saw Hallie and Sam Avery taking down the clothes that Hallie had washed that morning, and, as he passed the kitchen door, they both looked at him. Hallie had just reached up to unpin a shirt, and now her arms were arrested in mid-movement. As Calhoun moved up to her, she smiled and said, "You've thrown away your crutch, Keefe."

"About time, too. Has Weymarn been looking for me?"

Hallie shook her head, and now Calhoun looked over at Sam. There was much Calhoun wanted to tell Hallie, but in Sam's presence he knew he would have to keep silent.

Now Sam said, "What did you do with that hoe handle, Keefe? We could use it."

Calhoun eased himself down on the chopping block and said, "I left it past the Corners a ways. I'll ride out and get it if you want it."

Sam unpinned a shirt from the line and, tossing it into the basket, said, "You sure surprised Weymarn."

"How's that?" Calhoun asked.

"I was talking to him yesterday and he didn't believe you could ride a horse with your leg the way it was."

For a stunned moment Calhoun could not believe his ears and he was sure that the shock showed on his face. He looked at Hallie who was regarding Sam with open dismay.

"You mean you told him I was able to ride a horse?" Calhoun demanded.

Now Sam looked in puzzlement from Calhoun to Hallie, and then back to Calhoun. "Yes. Shouldn't I have?" When neither answered, Sam said, "He asked me if I'd really run your horse when I rode him and I told him that I really didn't get the horse to exercise him, but that I got him for you. I told you were trying to keep it a secret from Hallie because you were sure she wouldn't let you ride."

Hallie looked at Calhoun with consternation in her face.

"Did I do wrong?" Sam asked.

"No, Sam," Calhoun said quietly. So Weymarn did know that he could ride and that he had tried to keep the fact secret. Weymarn would know that there was only one reason for secrecy and he would conclude inevitably that his story of Wilkie Brown's death had been investigated.

Calhoun rose now and tramped over to the pump. He did not want Hallie watching him for he knew the alarm he felt could not be wholly hidden from her. Taking down the tin cup from its wire bale, he pumped a cup of water, and, turning his back to Hallie and Sam, he slowly sipped the water. Weymarn, he knew, would move against him now just as certainly as he had moved against Wilkie Brown.

Sam's innocent conversation had marked him for death. It would be easy enough for Weymarn to kill him; it would be as simple as waiting in the dark stable for him to come to bed, or having one of his men wait.

He had the cup to his lips when the thought came to him. How had Belle described Bolton, the man on the veranda? *The toughest hand Will's got.* Then why was Bolton in town now and why was Weymarn gone?

Patiently Calhoun recalled his conversation with Belle. Weymarn had lied about where he was going. Bolton had lied about seeing Weymarn, and Bolton, like all the Weymarn hands, would bunk in the stable overnight. The shape of it was plain enough, Calhoun saw. Weymarn had brought his toughest hand in to do a job he himself could never be accused of.

Calhoun threw out the remainder of the water and hung the cup back on its bale. Now everything was changed and his plans amounted to nothing. He couldn't work for Weymarn now. He heard Hallie saying, "Will you finish, Sam? I've got to start supper."

When Calhoun turned, Hallie was on her way to the kitchen and he knew this would probably be the only chance he would have to talk with her alone. He turned and followed her.

Calhoun stepped into the kitchen; Hallie, who was beginning to set the table, straightened up and looked at him.

"Well, Sam did it," Hallie said in a low voice.

"It wasn't his fault," Calhoun said. "It was mine for not telling him the whole truth."

"And mine. What will you do, Keefe?"

"Just be careful." He crossed to one of the chairs, pulled it out and slacked into it.

"Did you find out anything at the reservation?" Hallie asked.

"You might as well know it all, Hallie," Calhoun said. "Weymarn is holding Maco prisoner."

For a moment Hallie was speechless, her lips parted, her eyes wide in surprise. "Maco!" she echoed.

"Weymarn's got him and he's trying to sell him to Santiago's band. Weymarn sent Ryan to Santiago with the offer to return Maco for fifty head of horses and a hundred head of cattle. Santiago didn't have them and couldn't get them and he killed Ryan as an answer to Weymarn's offer." He paused. "I think Weymarn killed Wilkie Brown because Wilkie knew he held Maco and had talked."

Hallie stood motionless, unable to comprehend immediately the implications of Calhoun's news. "What will you do, Keefe?"

"Find Maco and take him back to Fort Kelso."

Hallie was silent a long minute. "You think Weymarn won't fight to keep him?"

"I know he will."

"You against every man that works for him!" Hallie cried.

Calhoun said quietly, "Two can play that game."

"One against twenty aren't very good odds, Keefe."

"Let it go, Hallie," Calhoun said wearily. And now, seeing the stubbornness in his face, Hallie turned to the stove.

"Anything happen while I was gone?"

"No," Hallie answered. Then she corrected herself. "The Army came through, is all."

"More of them chasing Maco?" Calhoun asked idly.

Hallie said, over her shoulder, "Dad said it was a detail headed for Silver City to escort the paymaster back to Fort Kelso. Dad said with only six men half a dozen of those Silver City toughs could take that payroll away from them."

Calhoun's attention sharpened. "Six men?"

"With one officer, Dad said. McKelway. Dad heard him talking to Weymarn and McKelway said two troops from Kelso are heading north and the rest are chasing Maco. I guess six men is all they could spare."

Calhoun came to his feet. *Only nine men,* he thought, *and Weymarn knows it.*

"Hallie," Calhoun said, unable to keep the excitement from his voice, "I think we've got it."

Hallie turned and looked at him, puzzlement in her face.

"That's why Weymarn went to the reservation to see Santiago. All Weymarn has to do is tell Santiago that the paymaster is carrying money. Santiago will attack the escort, and there's Maco's ransom money."

"Oh no," Hallie said in protest. "Nobody would do that!"

"Hallie, fix me up grub enough for a couple of days. I'm riding out right now."

"To where, Keefe?"

"To warn McKelway. If Santiago gets that payroll, then Maco's loose." He headed for the door. "I'll saddle up."

Stepping outside, Calhoun remembered that the saddle was still in the wash house where he had told Avery to put it, and now he turned and headed down the path. And then he remembered something else that brought him to an abrupt halt. Bolton would be looking for him and was waiting somewhere for his chance. A swift anger came to Calhoun and he thought, *I can be waiting, too.* He moved on now, a plan forming in his mind. Sam was just finishing taking down the clothes and now Calhoun halted by him. "Can you loan me your gun for a few minutes, Sam."

Avery's glance dropped to Calhoun's shell belt. "Yours broken?"

"Just a loan," Calhoun said insistently.

Puzzled, wanting to ask why he would need a gun anyway, Sam nevertheless lifted out his gun and handed it, butt first, to Calhoun.

Thanking him, Calhoun moved into the wash house and saw his saddle and blanket lying in a rear corner. Moving over to them, he untied his buckskin jacket from behind the candle and put it on. Then he lifted his own gun from its holster, rammed it in his belt and buttoned the jacket over it. Then he took off his shell belt, put Sam's gun in the holster, looped the shell belt over the saddle horn, picked up his saddle and bridle and moved outside.

Cutting across the back lots, he came alongside the stable and, moving across the stable lot, he halted at the corral. Then he swung his saddle, gun and shell belt dangling from its horn, onto the top pole of the corral, retaining only the bridle.

As he moved toward the gate, he looked about him and saw a man hunkered down against the stable wall. He was sifting dirt through his fingers and looking down so that his face was hidden by his hat brim. A faint excitement touched Calhoun; this was Bolton. What better way to keep track of a man's movements than watch his horse? Calhoun thought grimly.

Now Calhoun opened the corral gate and went inside. The horses there moved away from him, but his big chestnut slowly came toward him. Now Calhoun, back to the gate, was straightening the cheek strap before slipping the bit into the chestnut's mouth. As he did so he unbuttoned his jacket and made sure its skirt hid his gun.

"Didn't recognize you without the crutch," a voice said.

Calhoun turned slowly and there was Bolton standing some fifteen feet from him, hands on hips.

"Don't need it anymore," Calhoun said amiably.

Bolton took a quick look to his right and to his left, and then he said flatly, "That's my horse. Don't saddle him."

Here it is, Calhoun thought. "What if I do?" he asked softly.

"There's not much you can do. Your gun's on the fence."
Bolton was smiling and his hand started leisurely for the
gun in his holster.

All in one movement, Calhoun's hand swept under his
jacket skirt and came up with his gun, and now Bolton,
suddenly aware that he had been baited into a trap, streaked
for his gun.

He had it half out of its holster when Calhoun's gun finished its arc and went off.

Bolton was rammed swiftly backwards, his body like a
half-open jackknife and his gun went off in its holster. Five
feet from where he had been standing he landed on his back,
legs in the air, then rolled over on his side. One knee lifted
and then, accompanied by a shuddering groan, it fell, and he
was still.

Now Calhoun heard the sound of someone running.
Swiftly he put on the chestnut's bridle and led him past
Bolton toward the gate. He was opening it when the blacksmith hauled up just outside it, and now Calhoun let his
horse through.

"What happened?" the blacksmith asked.

"He claimed I was stealing his horse and pulled a gun on
me."

"But that's your horse," the blacksmith said.

"Yes." Calhoun moved around him, lifted his shell belt
from the saddle and was strapping it on when the first of the
three men who had run from the post at the sound of the
shot approached.

"What happened?" he asked.

"Ask the blacksmith," Calhoun said curtly. He threw the
saddle and blanket over the chestnut and was cinching up
when the two other men arrived.

He stepped into the saddle and put the chestnut in motion, and now he saw Belle Weymarn standing on the edge
of the loading platform. Cutting toward her, he reined in.

"Tell Will that Bolton wasn't the man for the job," Calhoun said thinly.

"You shot him?" Belle asked.

"Go look."

6

The days Hallie ironed were always the worst. To begin with the stove in the wash house had to be stoked unmercifully to heat the irons, and the room was stifling, making for short temper. Added to that, Cap and Sam Avery would not leave her alone. They had sat up until the small hours last night speculating on the reason for Calhoun killing a stranger. They had been at it again this morning, and now both of them had followed her into the wash house to continue their speculation. Both sat at the table where she wanted to lay her ironed clothes, cups of coffee before them, and she heard Cap talking.

"Figure it out for yourself," Cap said sourly. "He's never been any damned good. The Army fired him, didn't they?"

Sam glanced at Hallie and then said, "That's what you said," in a neutral voice.

"I'd like to know what really happened," Cap said for the fiftieth time. "No man is going to claim another man's horse in front of the man. You can't tell me that's the true story."

"But Tom Jeffers is no liar," Sam said stubbornly also for about the fiftieth time.

Hallie wished they would leave so that she could try to sort out her feelings. Only minutes after the gunshot last night, Keefe had ridden up and asked for the sack of grub. When Hallie, with Sam and Cap standing beside her, had asked him if he had heard the shot, he said, "It was mine. I killed a man who claimed my horse." He had reached for the sack of grub, had given Sam his gun, had touched his hat to her and then for all of them to hear, he had said, "Patience, Hallie" and had ridden off.

She gathered from the saloon talk Sam relayed to her last night that the man Calhoun killed was Wes Bolton, a tough employed by Weymarn at his ranch. Was this the first of Weymarn's many men who would try to get Keefe? In her own mind she was certain that Weymarn had put Bolton on Keefe and that he would keep putting others on him until he got him. Just the thought of it sickened her.

Cap was saying now, "Well there's our board money gone for good." He turned to Hallie. "Hallie, what did he mean when he said, 'Patience, Hallie'?"

"I told you a hundred times, I don't know," Hallie said, raw exasperation in her voice. But would he be back, Hallie wondered? How could he come back to Weymarn's town?

Now Cap rose, saying, "It's too hot in here." He plucked his shirt front away from his chest and was moving it, bellows fashion, to fan air against his thin body as he walked out the door.

Hallie moved to the stove, changed irons and came back to the ironing board, aware that Sam was watching her. This was the first time they had been alone since Calhoun had left, and Hallie dreaded more questioning.

Presently Sam said, "How have you really got this figured out, Hallie?"

Hallie sighed. "I've told you, I don't know, Sam."

"You were alone with him before he went over to the corral. Where was he riding to?"

"I can't tell you."

"Can't or won't?" Sam asked steadily.

Hallie's iron was suddenly still and she looked up at Sam. "I can tell you where he was going, but I won't. I can guess why he killed Bolton, but I won't tell you." Her voice held a real anger.

"Then you're hiding something from me, Hallie."

There was challenge in her voice as Hallie said, "Yes."

"Remember I'm the man that's going to be your husband," Sam said steadily.

Hallie, still looking at him, said, "Are you very sure of that?"

"Shouldn't I be?"

"How long has it been since you've thought to check on it?"

Sam looked puzzled. "Why, I don't remember."

"People change," Hallie said bitterly.

Sam thought a moment, then he said, "You mean people change people."

Hallie returned to her ironing now and said, "I don't understand that, Sam."

"Calhoun changed you."

Hallie shook her head. "No, he hasn't. You haven't bothered to ask me how I felt for over a year, Sam. You never gave me a ring that I could return to you. You never asked me, so I couldn't tell you."

"What have I done that's wrong, Hallie?"

"Nothing, nothing!" Hallie said vehemently. "You just take me for granted! You always have! Dad always has! I'm tired of it!"

"What do you want me to do?"

"Nothing now. It's too late. I just don't want to marry you, Sam. I haven't for over a year. It has nothing to do with Calhoun."

"It does," Sam contradicted flatly. "You're different when he's around. You're excited. You have secrets with him."

Hallie looked at him with searching eyes. "Yes. Have I ever had any secrets with you, Sam?"

"No."

Hallie's voice was soft. "I wonder why?" she asked.

Sam looked at her for a long moment and then rose. "I've

wondered, too." He passed her and went out into the sunlight.

The first day out of Silver City on the road back to Fort
Kelso, Lieutenant McKelway exercised the privilege of his
rank. He amiably ordered the enlisted man who was driver
for the paymaster, Lieutenant Wiegann, to take his horse,
and join the mounted troopers of the detail. He himself took
over the reins of the two teams hitched to the Douherty
wagon and drove. In the wagon he was shaded from the sun,
had congenial company and, leading the column, he and his
brother officer were out of the dust.

It was rolling foothill country that they were traveling
through and Lieutenant Wiegann, who had spent the last
two years of his Army career traveling from post to post
with the Army payroll, had discovered some of the amenities of his job. He carried a small-caliber shotgun with him,
and that afternoon he and McKelway amused themselves by
shooting quail that the Douherty wagon flushed.

In between shots McKelway leisurely caught up on the
careers of brother officers and their wives at other posts,
since Lieutenant Wiegann, by the very nature of his job, was
an encyclopedia of information within this department. He
was a first lieutenant and ten years McKelway's junior, a
dapper man, full of gossip and malice; and even though
McKelway knew he was being patronized by a younger senior officer, he was enjoying himself.

After an early start, they were past the outlying ranches
by mid-afternoon. The road now was empty of all traffic and
McKelway handed Wiegann the reins. He himself started
plucking the dozen quail which lay at his feet in the bed of
the Douherty wagon. Presently the detail labored to the
crest of the hill where Wiegann reined up to blow his teams.
Looking off across the flats below them that were shimmer-
ing crazily in the afternoon heat, Wiegann spotted the far
distant figure of a single rider. Calling McKelway's atten-

tion to it, he said, "There's a brave man, or a fool. Probably an Indian though."

This reminded McKelway of the death of Ryan, and as the Douherty wagon got underway again, he told Wiegann of the butchery. They discussed the Apache situation in general and presently they became interested in the approaching rider. As the rider neared, they saw he was a tall man on a big chestnut horse, and now McKelway, frowning, said, "I've seen him around Kelso."

The rider pulled his horse off the road and reined up, lazily lifting a hand as if requesting them to halt, and Wiegann pulled in his teams.

McKelway, remembering, said now, "You're Keefe Calhoun, aren't you?"

"That's right, Lieutenant."

"You were guiding Lieutenant Benson when he got jumped, weren't you?"

Calhoun nodded.

"Heading for Silver City?"

"No, I guess I was heading for you," Calhoun replied.

McKelway smiled faintly, "Well you've found us. What's on your mind?"

Calhoun's face was powdered with fine dust, and now he took his neckerchief and wiped his face. McKelway saw him looking at Wiegann and he got the impression that the man was having a hard time framing what he wanted to say.

Calhoun finally spoke. "Lieutenant, I think you're headed for a scrap with the Apaches."

McKelway looked at Wiegann, then back to Calhoun. "You have information?"

"Not direct, no. Indirectly, yes."

"What does that mean?" McKelway asked bluntly.

"I can't tell you exactly, but the information is accurate enough. Santiago's friends are going to break off the reservation to head for Mexico. That payroll you're carrying will buy horses and food across the border."

Wiegann said drily, "Since when did an Apache buy a horse? I always thought they stole them."

Calhoun said nothing, only watched the two men with patience. McKelway frowned now. "Let's get this straight. You have information that we might be jumped for our money by Santiago's band?"

Calhoun nodded.

"But you can't tell us where you got the information?" McKelway went on.

"That's it."

McKelway felt a faint anger stirring within him. Was he supposed to credit every wild rumor that was picked up? He said drily, "Paymasters have been traveling across this country since the military first moved in, but I've never heard of the Apaches attacking a paymaster's escort. Have you?"

"No," Calhoun said.

McKelway scowled. "If I believed your story, just what do you propose I do?"

"Go back to Silver City and get more men. You're authorized to pay them in an emergency, aren't you?"

"That's something that's never come up," McKelway said drily. "We're supposed to protect civilians; they're not supposed to protect us."

"You can pay for civilian guides," Calhoun pointed out.

McKelway nodded. "Suppose I got more men and I wasn't jumped? The major wouldn't honor my requisition and it would come out of my pay for the next seventy years, if I were around that long."

"Then send to Fort Kelso for more men."

McKelway said coldly, "If they thought I needed more men, they'd have given 'em to me."

Calhoun's voice was dry as he said, "You can sure prove them wrong by losing your whole detail."

"You guided for Benson, you said?" McKelway remarked.

Calhoun nodded.

"The stage driver brought Benson's report to Kelso after that first attack." He paused. "Benson blamed you and you alone. He would have dropped you even if you hadn't been hurt."

"He dropped me because I warned an Apache camp of his attack. He destroyed the camp and the attack on us was retaliation."

"In situations like that," McKelway said slowly, "it's always nice to get both versions. However, Benson's report holds you unreliable and incompetent."

"My report on Benson would say about the same thing," Calhoun said quietly.

McKelway said angrily, "Unfortunately you report to nobody but yourself, Calhoun."

Calhoun held his silence and now McKelway looked at Wiegann. The senior lieutenant had an amused smile on his face and now he said slyly, "A dilemma, eh?"

McKelway knew that Wiegann, who outranked him, would not offer a comment of any sort: he, McKelway, was in command of the escort. Now McKelway looked at Calhoun and when he spoke his voice held contempt. "Calhoun, you just presented me with an unprovable rumor that you picked up God knows where. On the strength of it, I do not propose to turn tail and run back to Silver City. Nor do I propose to make camp, fortify it and send for help. My orders are to escort the paymaster from Silver City to Fort Kelso with the detail provided. I propose to do just that."

Calhoun nodded. "If you've got good sense, Lieutenant, then you'll put out flankers and use some caution."

McKelway's temper flared. "Are you telling me how to handle my detail?"

"I guess I am," Calhoun said slowly. "This is a little different than taking a Sunday drive in a buggy."

"It's a great sport for you civilians, this giving advice to the Army. Still, we've been around for a while and we'll be around after you're dead. Now, stand back."

With that McKelway reached for the reins in Wiegann's

hand, turned and ordered his men, who had been indifferently watching the conference, into motion. Now McKelway turned to Wiegann and said angrily, "Of all the damned insolence."

"These civilians can always do it better, can't they?" Wiegann observed. Then he asked idly, "Think there's anything in what he said?"

"I do not," McKelway said flatly. "You've been a paymaster for some time. Have you ever been attacked by the Indians?"

"No, and I refuse to think there'll always be a first time," Wiegann said drily.

"This man is thoroughly unreliable," McKelway said grimly. "He knows the country and he knows the Apaches, but I sometimes wonder if he isn't working for them instead of us." He related then the information that Lieutenant Benson's dispatch to Major Burns had carried. He finished by saying, "Benson had to pick up a new guide at Weymarn's Crossing. I dare say the new one is as bad as Calhoun was." He paused and then said one word which might as well have been an obscenity, "Civilians."

Later that afternoon McKelway noticed that Calhoun had turned around and was following the detail at the distance of half a mile or so. He made up his mind that he would not welcome Calhoun into their camp that night. No man was going to insult him and then claim Army protection.

It was almost evening when McKelway turned the Douherty wagon off the main road and onto a faint wagon road. A half mile down it they came to a small adobe building with close by a caved-in corral and pole shed whose roof had fallen in. It was named on Army maps as Courtland's ranch, and it was so small and so isolated that no owner had ever been able to defend it against Apache marauders. Because of this it was long since abandoned, and the only reason it graced military maps was because here in this vast dryness was water.

McKelway set a pair of troopers to filling the corral tank with water from a pump in the yard. The horses were rubbed down and grained and by that time the detail had two fires going, a big one for the enlisted men and a separate fire set at a distance for the two officers. The horses were put on a picket line before dark and as McKelway set about preparing the quail supper, he put out a guard.

When he and Wiegann had fired up their after-dinner cigars and were sharing the whisky from Wiegann's flask, the troopers were rolling into their blankets. McKelway went over to the enlisted men's fire and hauled up. "Corporal Nelson, double the guard tonight and change it every two hours. I want you on the guard change at daylight."

The corporal nodded somberly. The quail supper, washed down by whisky and topped off by cigars, had not gone unnoticed by the troopers. And while they were used to officers enjoying certain prerogatives, they, like all the common soldiers in recorded history, resented them.

McKelway returned to his own fire where he and Wiegann finished their nightcaps. Wiegann stared into the darkness at the adobe building which was faintly illuminated by the troopers' dying fire. "Do we bunk in there?"

"Not on your life," McKelway said flatly. "There are scorpions, snakes, and spiders in there unto the tenth generation. I won't fight them over it."

He and Wiegann threw their blankets on the ground and by silent agreement put their guns at the head of their blankets. McKelway pulled off his boots, arranged his saddle for a pillow and rolled into the blankets. Wiegann was already hunched in his blankets under the Douherty wagon, his back to the fire. Now McKelway smoked the last of his cigar and pitched it toward the fire. Mentally he checked back to see if he had taken every precaution. He knew he had, and now his thoughts turned to Calhoun. The Army, he thought, had an answer to everything, even to the Calhouns of this world.

McKelway was wakened at bare dawn by a scream that

brought him up on all fours, reaching for his gun. He had time to see the swarm of Apaches descending afoot on the still prone troopers; he even had time to hear stampeding horses from the picket line before he took the Apache lance through his back. He even had time to look between his arms and see where the lance had come through his body, its point buried in the ground. The rest was fading fear and panic and pain into welcome blackness.

When Calhoun reached the Crossing sometime after midnight he let his horse drink from the stream and then moved deep into the cottonwood motte where he picketed the chestnut, rubbed him down and gave him the last of the grain. The settlement was dark and he wondered how he could waken Hallie without alarming her.

Weymarn was probably back and would be hunting him, Calhoun knew; he might even have a man posted to watch the Thompson house. Still, Calhoun knew he must take the risk, for Hallie was important to his plans now. He waded the creek and drifted into the deep shadow of the dark cabin. Halting at the rear corner he waited for minutes, listening, watching, and when he could hear only the normal night sounds he moved up and knocked softly and persistently on the door. Presently, he heard Hallie's muffled voice calling, "Who is it?"

"Me. Keefe."

"Just a minute."

He waited a moment, saw a crack of light show under the door and then he heard the bolt shot and the door was opened. Hallie, wearing a black, full-sleeved wrapper, belted at the waist, moved back a step into the room and Calhoun came through the door. Suddenly Hallie moved toward him, put both her hands on his shoulders and buried her face in his chest. Touching her, Calhoun felt her trembling, and now she said softly, "Oh, Keefe, I knew you'd come back!"

"Did you think I wouldn't?" Calhoun asked gently.

"Oh, I knew it, but still I didn't. They all said you wouldn't."

The voice came from the bedroom door, "I said you wouldn't."

Hallie backed away abruptly and now Calhoun saw Cap, pants pulled over his underwear, standing in the doorway, his rifle held at ready. "Bolton died."

"He was dead when I left him, Cap."

"You've got Weymarn to answer to," Cap said sourly.

"I know."

"I don't want you to hang around this place," Cap continued. "You'll bring him down on us."

"I know that, too, Cap. Now go to bed. I want to talk to Hallie."

Calhoun watched him stand there, undecided a moment, before he turned and went back into his room. Now Calhoun looked at Hallie, and he saw that her face was still sober and worried.

"Was Bolton brought in to kill you, Keefe?"

Calhoun only nodded.

"He's only the first one," Hallie said bitterly. "There'll be others."

"I got past Bolton, didn't I?"

Hallie sighed. "One isn't twenty." She turned away. "Let me start a fire, Keefe. I'll get you something to eat."

"I can't stay, Hallie. I'd better keep moving."

"Did you reach McKelway?"

"I talked with him," Calhoun said, and a faint bitterness crept into his voice. "He told me to mind my own business."

"You think they'll be attacked?"

"I think what I've always thought, that the payroll will wind up with Weymarn. I think we'll know when the stage comes through tomorrow."

"Can't we send help, Keefe?"

"This is Weymarn's town. Would he send it? Who'd ask for help? Me?" He shook his head. "No, Hallie, let's just hope I'm wrong."

"What will you do now, Keefe? You can't stay here."

"Get Maco back."

"You keep saying that, but how, how?" Hallie said vehemently.

"If the escort's attacked and the money's taken, Weymarn's got to deliver Maco. I follow him to Maco."

"But how do you follow him if you're hiding in the hills?"

"Who said I'd be in the hills?"

Hallie looked at him in puzzlement. "Where will you be?"

"Under Weymarn's loading platform."

Hallie said, "Oh, no." It was almost a moan. "You can't mean that!"

"Can you think of a better place to hide than the loading platform, Hallie? It's closed in. I can look out into the corral where Weymarn keeps his horses. I'll know when he rides out if it's day or night. If you'll give me a couple of days' grub, I'll go tonight, Hallie."

Hallie moved over to the cabinet and took out a loaf of bread, and Calhoun wearily slacked into one of the chairs. Now Hallie brought the bread over to the table, sliced it and began to make cold meat sandwiches. Her eyes were brooding as she glanced over at Calhoun now. "How will you follow him without a horse?"

"I left mine picketed deep in the cottonwoods across the stream, Hallie. Can you ask Sam to grain him tomorrow?"

"I'll do it myself."

"Why can't Sam?"

"I don't think he'll be around anymore, Keefe. He left for Kelso today to look for a job."

Calhoun watched her a moment, then asked curiously, "Why does that embarrass you, Hallie?"

She looked up quickly. "Does it show that much? All right, we quarreled. He wanted me to marry him right away."

"You didn't want to?"

"I—told him I'd never marry him."

Calhoun felt a quiet elation and he said, "Did you ever think you would? I didn't."

Hallie's hands stilled and she looked soberly at him. "Why didn't you?"

Calhoun's voice was gentle as he said, "Because it's me you'll marry, Hallie. You had to settle this business with Sam yourself first, but it's me you'll marry."

Calhoun rose, came over and put both hands on her shoulders and turned her to face him.

"You sound awful sure of yourself," Hallie said quietly.

Calhoun smiled. "If you won't marry me, Hallie, you'll be stuck with me anyway. As long as you take in boarders, you'll have me underfoot. When you quit, I'll move in next door. When you move away I'll move with you. Whatever you do and wherever you go you'll be stuck with me, Hallie. Would you want that?"

Hallie smiled shyly. "I don't know."

"You'd better know when I get back, Hallie, because that's when I start sticking."

Calhoun heard a movement and looked up to find Cap standing in the bedroom door.

"Both times I've seen you tonight you've had your hands on Hallie. Take them off!" Cap's voice was rough.

"Just one minute, Cap," Calhoun said. He leaned down and kissed Hallie on the lips, then looked up at Cap, took his hands off Hallie's shoulders and said, "All right."

Cap stared in stunned silence for a moment and then said sharply, "Hallie!"

Calhoun looked at Hallie who raised her hand now and touched her lips with the tip of her fingers. Now she looked up at Calhoun and he saw the tenderness in her eyes. Then slowly, deliberately, she turned to face her father. "I wanted him to," she said quietly.

"Calhoun, get out of this house!" Cap said.

"Right away," Calhoun said amiably.

"And don't come back!" Cap said grimly.

"We'll talk about that later," Calhoun said, still amiably.

Hallie moved over to the cabinet, got a newspaper and deftly wrapped up the sandwiches which Calhoun put in his pocket. As he moved toward the door, Hallie said quietly, "Do come back," and smiled.

Calhoun stepped out into the night, and he felt a wild elation which, he reflected wryly, was a strange thing in a mature man. Had he intended tonight to ask Hallie to marry him, he wondered? He knew he hadn't. There had been the hope in the back of his mind that Hallie would some day recognize Sam Avery for what he was, a dull, plodding, thickheaded man who deserved a dull, plodding and thickheaded wife. But Hallie had surprised him and in that surprise he had asked her. It would have come some time, but he had never imagined it would come so soon.

He cut quietly through the back lots and halted at the corner of the stable. He could not see a single light anywhere and now, almost reluctantly, he moved toward the loading platform. He guessed that it might be a couple of hours till daylight, but he could not risk being picked up by some late riders or early risers. He approached the platform, felt along the boards for the door and then remembered the baskets of empty bottles that he must avoid. On all fours then he moved inside, pulled the door behind him, skirted the baskets and found a cleared space where he could stretch out, his head toward the corral.

Lying on his back, he tried for the sleep which would not come. He was thinking of Hallie and the kind of life he could show her. He would take her away from this accursed place and she would never take in another washing or sell another loaf of bread. He remembered a small ranch in the White Mountains to the north where, when these troubles were over and he had a small stake, he could build a cabin and break remounts for the horse-hungry Army. It was. . . .

A new and strange sound came to him and he raised his head. It was a quiet scuffing of something climbing the loading platform steps. He peered out through a crack in the warped boards and saw nothing but the deep blackness of the night. Dust from the cracks of the platform above him sifted down on his neck, and he listened so intently that he heard his own pulse hammering. The scuffing moved away from him across the platform. A wandering dog, he wondered?

There was a moment of utter silence and then he heard several soft thudding sounds that seemed to come from inside the store. He waited and then there came the scuffing sounds again. Then he heard a word softly spoken, *"Enju."*

Now he felt his heart leap. This was the Apache word for, "It is well." But who spoke the word? Were the Apaches, under cover of darkness, prowling the town before they struck?

Now the scuffing came again and he knew now that he had been listening to the whisper of moccasins as they crossed the platform and went down the steps. Then the earth absorbed all sound and Calhoun lay there, waiting, trying to puzzle this out. Minutes passed without a sound and now, curiosity pushing him, Calhoun quietly moved to the door, pushed it open and stood up in the night. Still no sound. Had they been trying to get into the post through the rear door? Calhoun turned and softly climbed the steps, crossed the platform and halted at the door. It was locked, of course, but the faint thuds he had heard seemed to come from inside the post. Gently then he tried the latch and to his surprise it lifted and released. Quietly Calhoun pushed the door open and stepped inside into the utter blackness of the big room.

What was he looking for and what did he think he could see? Recklessly then he reached in his pocket, drew out a match and wiped it alight on the wall. By its quick flare he saw the canvas sacks on the floor leaning against the wall. There were four of them, and now in caution he doused the match. Moving toward the sacks he knelt and felt of them. Under his fingers were the hard forms of coins, and he heard the unmistakable clink of gold coin on gold coin.

Understanding came to him then with a swift and terrible knowledge. This was the payroll that McKelway's escort had been guarding. It meant that the detail had been attacked and probably wiped out, since the chest ironed to the Dougherty wagon would have had to be captured and broken open. Santiago, undoubtedly through necessity, had been made to deliver the money to the place specified by Weymarn. That would have been here at the post at night. For if Weymarn had agreed to any other place, the Apaches would have followed him from the cache to Maco. And, once Maco was in their hands, they would have killed him. Weymarn had left the rear door open for the delivery and since he opened the store each morning, it was he who would first see the gold and hide it before opening the store.

Now Calhoun rose and quietly moved back to the door, opened it, stepped out into the night and closed the door behind him. This made his task easier, he knew. Instead of having to wait under the platform to spot Weymarn and follow him, he would have a head start. Weymarn undoubtedly would move today. If Wilkie Brown had been headed for Maco's hiding place when he was killed, then the hiding place lay somewhere to the west of the rock-floored mesa where Wilkie's body had been found. Calhoun could watch the break in the canyon rim for Weymarn.

Moving away from the post, Calhoun cut through the back lots, through the Thompson back yard and crossed the stream. In the cottonwood thicket he saddled his horse. He turned to the stream to let his horse drink and filled his canteen and then headed south. ·

The sun was an hour high when Calhoun broke through the break in the canyon rim and turned east, traveling almost a half-mile through the piñons and cedars before he reined in and dismounted. He tied his chestnut back from the rim and then moved to the edge of the cap rock where he could look down at the road snaking across the low hills to climb the mesa. It was another cloudless day and the coolness of the night was receding under the brass-bright sun.

As he waited, Calhoun wondered if his reasoning had been wrong. Maybe Weymarn, made cautious by his suspicion that Calhoun had scouted the mesa after Wilkie's death, had shifted Maco. Still, that seemed improbable. Weymarn had called Bolton in to take care of Calhoun. When Bolton was killed Weymarn was away at the agency. If Maco had been moved then it would have had to have been yesterday after Weymarn returned. But Weymarn, knowing that no man could singlehandedly search these mountains, would have probably taken the chance and left Maco where he was.

Calhoun's lack of sleep was catching up with him, and now, looking down at the country before him and seeing it empty, he rose and tramped back into the timber to keep himself awake. When he returned minutes later he saw the tiny distant figure of a horseman. As it grew nearer Calhoun called on an iron patience. This might not be Weymarn and Weymarn might never come, but as the figure crossed below him on the road to the switchbacks that climbed the mesa, Calhoun breathed a sigh of relief. The wide, deep-chested figure could never be mistaken for another rider. It was Weymarn.

Calhoun waited in the still morning. He knew that Weymarn, once he achieved the rim, would halt a long time to rest his horse and watch his backtrail. Calhoun watched it, too. The fact that Weymarn had come alone puzzled him for a moment, then he realized that Maco had been fed and guarded and Weymarn must have men at the hiding place.

He gave Weymarn a full hour, which would allow him his look at the backtrail and again his look back at the mesa before he started his climb into the foothills to the mountains beyond. Calhoun could scarcely contain his patience as he finally mounted and rode back to the road, crossed it and continued east. If there were fresh tracks on the old ones that climbed to the foothills, Calhoun would know he was headed right, but by now it was too late for him to do anything about it.

Where the foothill trail rose off the mesa, Calhoun saw new tracks. He pulled off the trail, then, paralleling it, every half-hour returning to it to confirm that Weymarn had passed.

He was well above the farthest point he had come before, and now the thick piñons and cedars were giving way to taller timber. Calhoun waited until he was in the big timber before cutting back to pick up Weymarn's tracks again. When he came to the trail he reined in and studied it, and as it yielded its message he felt his spine tingle. Here were Weymarn's tracks, but over them were the tracks of two unshod ponies.

The Apaches, then, were also trailing Weymarn.

Calhoun pulled his horse around and went back down the trail and within a few minutes he saw where the two Apache ponies had come out of the canyon. He knew the Apache habit of traveling a parallel canyon, crossing the trail only at intervals to make sure they had not lost their quarry. Once they were certain of the direction their victim was traveling, they would circle ahead and wait in ambush. Today, however, Calhoun was sure there would be no ambush until Weymarn had led them to Maco.

Now he turned and rode back up the trail, pushing his tired horse. Instead of one man to watch out for, he now had three. The trail threaded the tall timber along the shoulder of the canyon, then cut through a wide meadow, which Calhoun skirted cautiously, keeping to the timber. Picking up the trail on the far side of the meadow, he reined in again. Now, instead of horse tracks covering Weymarn's tracks, there were two sets of moccasin tracks. Calhoun knew that the Apaches, sensing that they were close to Weymarn and knowing that their horses were cumbersome for stalking, had left them back in the timber. They were probably afoot paralleling the trail and right now they could even be ahead of Weymarn.

Recklessly then, Calhoun determined to hold to the trail. He drew his rifle from its boot and rode on, rifle across his saddle.

The trail began to dip into a timbered canyon and Calhoun saw that following it would expose him to a watcher on the far side of the canyon. He came to his decision then, and rode deep into the timber, dismounted, tied his chestnut and then, staying well away from the trail, moved steadily into the canyon, the soft humus of pine needles deadening the small sounds he could not avoid making.

He walked thus for ten minutes and then cut back to the trail, but before he reached it he pulled up behind a tree, and looked across and down the canyon. There on a cleared shelf across the canyon he saw the roof of a shack and the head frame of a mine shaft. Moving closer to the trail, he could see where it achieved the bottom of the canyon and then swung back with a lift to the cabin. Was this Weymarn's destination?

Fading back into the timber, he moved on, aiming for the switchback and, minutes later, as cautiously as possible, he achieved the valley floor and cut back to the trail. Here was the track of Weymarn's horse climbing the two hundred yards to the cabin, but the moccasin tracks were not there.

Calhoun was certain that the trailing Apaches, faced with this situation, would divide forces, swinging wide so that they could approach from either side to survey the ground. Recklessly, he decided that he would take up his station between the two of them. Now, keeping barely out of sight of the trail, he moved up the timbered slope, pausing occasionally to listen. Presently, he could see the break in the timber ahead of him and the ground began to level off. Now, bending over, he moved from tree to tree until, through the remaining timber, he saw the cabin.

And then what he saw made him sink to the ground and flatten himself. In front of the cabin Weymarn had tied his horse to a splinter of stump. Behind and to the right of the cabin was the high head frame astride a mine shaft.

Weymarn and another man, who wore range clothes and a black hat so old it was faded to green, were just finishing lowering a ladder into the shaft. A rope had been tied around the head of the ladder and now as it disappeared into the shaft, Weymarn's helper seized the rope, backed off, braced himself and played out a few feet of the rope as the ladder descended.

Now Weymarn backed off, palming up his gun as he did so. This, then, was where Maco had been kept hidden. Slowly Calhoun looked about him, knowing that the two Apaches were watching this, too. Then his attention returned to the head frame. Calhoun could see Weymarn's helper bracing himself as weight was put on the rope. Then a dark arm appeared, grasping the rope on the lip of the shaft. Another arm appeared, then a dark head with a bright flannel headband. Now Weymarn backed off a step and Maco pulled himself over the lip of the mine shaft and came slowly to his feet. He was wearing a cast-off coat and breechclout; the legging on his left leg had rolled down and Calhoun saw the rags that were tied about his calf and lower thigh.

Weymarn said something to him and Maco started toward the cabin. Weymarn's helper had also drawn his gun and now, with Maco ahead of them, he and Weymarn moved toward the shack, Maco walking with a deep limp. Alongside the shack Maco slowly turned, leaned on the shack and started to speak. Cautiously Weymarn came closer and he, too, put his shoulder against the shack wall.

There followed a long discussion, with Maco doing the talking and with Weymarn shaking his head in negation. Calhoun's glance shifted to Weymarn's horse. The horse had turned its head and, ears up, was watching the timber on the canyon side, and Calhoun guessed that the horse had caught a movement or scent of one of the hidden Apaches.

Now the conversation came to an end. Maco turned and limped past the corner of the cabin toward the trail. Calhoun thought grimly, *What do I do now?* Here was Maco, apparently free, and Calhoun knew that his discussion with Weymarn had been over a mount which Weymarn had denied him. Calhoun knew it would be certain death to try to capture Maco now in front of Weymarn and his man. It would be equally certain death to wait until Maco was down the trail and then capture him, for the two Apaches would be on him.

Maco, under the watchful attention of Weymarn and his man, passed Weymarn's horse, and now a sudden movement in the timber to his right caught Calhoun's attention. He turned his head just in time to see an Apache seemingly rise out of the ground at the edge of the timber. In one fluid movement he threw his lance. It traveled with an impossibly flat projectory and only at the last second did Weymarn hear anything. He pushed away from the wall and turned toward the sound just in time to catch the lance square in his chest. The driving lance went clear through Weymarn and the point buried itself in the log wall.

The thud of it, along with Weymarn's throttled cry, turned Weymarn's helper around. He saw the Apache, who now was racing toward him. With a quickness Calhoun could scarcely follow, the man got off two shots. The first stopped the Apache as if he had run into a wall; the second knocked him flat on his back.

Three things then happened at once. Maco fell flat on his face, seeking the cover of the weeds and grass; the second Apache boiled out of the timber on the far side of the trail and Weymarn's helper doubtless thinking he was being attacked by a whole band, snapped a shot in the oncoming Apache and raced for the door of the cabin.

The Apache held a rifle in his left hand and a pistol in his right. As he raced past Maco, he dropped the rifle alongside Maco. He was weaving and bobbing, running for the protection of Weymarn's horse, and now he snapped a shot at the white man. Weymarn's helper paused beside the door, carefully took aim and fired and the Apache went down. Now the white man whirled and had the door half open when

Maco's rifle slammed out. The slug caught the white man square in the back and he pitched through the door face down.

Calhoun, already on his feet, lunged through the last of the timber as Maco came erect.

"Maco!" he called sharply.

The Apache chief turned swiftly, and now Calhoun, his rifle at ready, said, in Apache, "Put it down."

Maco shot from the hip and then turned and staggered toward Weymarn's horse.

Calhoun raised his rifle, shot over Maco's head and yelled, "Stop!" When Maco did not hesitate, Calhoun levered in a fresh shell, aimed at his legs and fired.

Maco went down in a rolling fall and came to his feet immediately. He was facing Calhoun now and in the one brief instant they looked at each other across the thirty yards of ground that lay between them, Calhoun knew Maco was no longer running; he was fighting. Calhoun lunged to his right as Maco's gun was lifted again and he fired, and before Calhoun was pushing himself to his knees Maco was charging. Abandoning his rifle, Calhoun's hand streaked for his holster. Maco, in a limping run, was charging, levering in a shell as he ran.

Calhoun lifted his pistol, sighted at Maco's highest bandage and fired, rolling to his left as he saw Maco stagger and shoot into the air as he fell. Now Calhoun, his legs driving under him, came to his feet, running for Maco. The Apache chief, in falling, had somehow contrived to face Calhoun. And now Calhoun heard the shell levered in and saw the rifle rise and the face behind it, contorted with pain and rage. There was no capturing Maco now, Calhoun knew.

Halting, Calhoun lifted his gun, making himself wait that part of a second that it took to bring Maco's head into his sight, and then he fired.

He saw Maco's face dissolve; he saw the body jar roughly and then Maco, face down, was still.

* * *

It was mid-day when Calhoun rode into Weymarn's Crossing leading Weymarn's horse with the older man's tarp-wrapped body tied across the saddle. Before he had reached the post tie rail, men were running toward him. And now, reaching the post, he wearily swung out of the saddle. Turning, looking across his saddle at the post door, he saw Belle Weymarn framed in it. Slowly he took off his hat, moved around his horse and climbed the veranda steps.

Weymarn's body had been wrapped so that it was impossible to tell what the tarp contained, but Belle, seeing Calhoun remove his hat and recognizing her husband's horse, did not need to be told. There was a bitter sadness in her face as Calhoun halted before her.

"Will?" she asked.

Calhoun only nodded. "Maco got him," Calhoun said slowly.

"Not you then?"

"No." He wondered if he had to explain more, but he knew that he did. Somewhere in the post was an Army payroll and Belle would have to know everything. That, however, could wait. He only said, so that people gathered around could hear him, "There'll be time later to tell you, Belle."

He turned and was headed for the steps when Belle said, "Keefe, did he bring it on himself?"

Calhoun turned, watched her a moment, and then said quietly, "Yes, all of it."

Weymarn's horse with its burden had already been led down the alley toward the stables when Calhoun took the trailing reins of his horse and afoot set out for the Thompsons'. Cap, he saw, was in the crowd that had gathered on the veranda.

He was halfway to the Thompsons' when he saw Hallie's slight figure come out the gate, start for him, and then hesitate.

She was waiting when Calhoun came up and halted before her.

"Starting today you won't be rid of me, Hallie, remember?"

Hallie smiled her shy smile. "I was on my way to remind you."